BOOKS BY STEVEN SHER

POETRY
Trolley Lives (Wampeter Press)
Caught In The Revolving Door (Love Street Books)
Persnickety (Seven Woods Press)
Nickelodeon (Gull Books)

NON-FICTION
Northwest Variety: Personal Essays By 14 Regional Authors (Co-editor; Arrowood Books)

Man With A Thousand Eyes AND Other Stories

Steven Sher

GULL BOOKS

Copyright © 1989 by Steven Sher
All Rights Reserved

The author wishes to thank the following publications where these stories first appeared: "Beasts" (*Ascent*); "Harvest of Gould" (*Ball State University Forum*); "Silverman's Tomb" (*Confrontation*); "Lovers" (*Long Pond Review*); "Spare Rib Park" (*The Louisville Review*); "Man With A Thousand Eyes" (*Reconstructionist*); "Pigeon Soup" (appeared as "Who Shall Live and Who Shall Die" in *Skyline*).

First Printing, 1989
Book And Cover Design By Nancy Green Sher
ISBN 0-940584-17-4

GULL BOOKS
Little Westkill Road
R.R. 1, Box 273A
Prattsville, New York 12468

*For
Uncle Max*

Contents

Introduction	9
Beasts	15
Spare Rib Park	23
Lovers	33
Pigeon Soup	43
Man With A Thousand Eyes	51
Harvest Of Gould	59
Rainbow Man	67
The Tenth Plague	75
Silverman's Tomb	85

INTRODUCTION

A terrible absence haunts these nine stories of twentieth-century Jewish life, and that absence prevails in the larger American culture. The stories seek out that absence as the tongue seeks the damaged and potentially painful tooth. The absence is the more terrible because Sher does not thrust it forward for the reader to observe and deplore. Instead, the absence is a given, one of the necessary facts out of which the stories operate. When, as sometimes occurs, wry humor accompanies the absence, the humor does not provide relief. It exacerbates.

To a man, woman, and child, the people in Sher's stories lack contexts in which to find or to express love. They lack personal significance, and their strategies to fill their lacks are almost exactly as grotesque as the strategies by which most Americans in the latter half of the twentieth century cheer themselves up in order to muddle through. The surface tensions of Sher's stories derive from those matters of fact which bind human lives together in parodies of living; beneath those tensions, gape cavities which draw everything and everybody toward them.

For the most part, the stories in *Man With A Thousand Eyes* do not include instances of wilful wrongdoing. People do the things they do simply because those are the things they do, and Sher's prose style, his way of telling, is quietly suited to his actions. The central character in the collection's final and possibly best story, "Silverman's Tomb," commits a repugnant crime, but the reader learns of it through indirection and it becomes yet another of the details entrapping the narrator in a meaningless, absurd existence. In "The Tenth Plague," a drunken rape, motivated and narrated in less than a page, seems as inevitable as it is brutal. The rapist's hands, Sher tells the reader, "were all over her as he forced her into the darkening house." To the victim, the rape "felt like seeping darkness." The violent action grows naturally from the story's earlier events, and the even more violent retribution, precisely because it descends mysteriously and matter of factly, seems entirely plausible.

"The Tenth Plague" focuses on Rozie, a delicatessen owner in a changing New York neighborhood. Starker, "the developer's firstborn," baits Rozie in his efforts to get her to sell her property. The arrival of Rozie's cousin, "a small Jew from Safed," provokes curiosity and increases business. Starker taunts the new-comer, calls him Moses, and says he looks more like an accountant than like Charlton Heston. Starker's rape of Dina, the daughter of the only other Jewish business family in the neighborhood, results in Starker's physical torment. Sher writes that the hell Starker housed "burned for release from every pore, like open wounds that drained his life." His sight is gone, he streams with blood, and "his memory of recent events left him no peace." Though the story links Starker's punishment to Rozie's cousin, she and her retarded son remain aliens in the old neighborhood and the reader recalls Starker's statement to her: "Jews run from a neighborhood faster than anyone." Rozie's family business, her waiter Sid, and her few remaining regular customers represent an effort to maintain community, something like a context to live in, but that context erodes.

Goldstein in the title story has been in Brooklyn almost sixty years, but "his context is from the preceding score." As much as any other character, Goldstein epitomizes the absence which haunts contemporary life. "For most of three-quarters of a century, Goldstein has spoken alarmingly of death...'I don't believe in miracles,' he says, 'except I always seem to make it to another day.'" The narrator observes, "As long as he complains, he'll never die. So it is that Goldstein's getting younger." The crazy logic is irrefutable.

Goldstein jokes, he insults his wife, he pinches his grandchildren. He is a coward whose broken finger is a trophy of that cowardice: he smashed his finger with a loose stone from a synagogue to make himself useless as a soldier in Poland. Although he has always feared the man with a thousand eyes, he suggests ironically that his wife may be interested in a proposition from Death. By the end of the story, Hannah, the long-suffering wife, overhearing only her husband's half of a telephone conversation, which seems to provide evidence that he has another woman, "turns away, following the flight of thoughts beyond this life, beyond the room."

All of Sher's stories achieve complexity without being complicated, and they are subtle, even ambiguous without being confused. They allow the reader to observe the strategies of people trying to make, or to retain, something meaningful in their lives. Some of the characters are obsessed—a woman devotes all her energies to keeping a cat alive and a man gardens fiercely and ardently in the sight of his dying wife. Another man, recovering from bullet wounds, slips past his wife to return to his unnecessary, unrewarding work.

"Spare Rib Park," one of two first-personal stories, is among the most complex of the stories. In it, a young man confuses his emergent erotic needs and the forbidden taste of take-out food from a Chinese restaurant. Although when the narrator's grandparents stepped off the boat, "they still kept kosher," the grandmother soon begins to deceive her orthodox husband and gives her grandson a plate of spare ribs. The boy boasts of his courting technique based on carry-out spare ribs eaten in a park where he carves the initials of successive young women on a wooden bench. After a humiliating failure with one date, he plans another date which will begin with his initiating the girl "with an unkosher kiss, from sticky ribs." By then, Grandma was dying in the hospital, and the narrator thinks he would be willing to sacrifice even his Saturday nights for her, though he knows "she'd never ask me to give up anything for her."

> If only I could find a girl who would be satisfied so easily, not even spare ribs would be necessary. My appetite would be satisfied for all time, for all nights, without the words and kisses that promised more than

someone eventually gave.

In the park, the young man thinks of his unsatisfactory date, imagining her waiting by the telephone ready to jump at his offer of spare ribs. All around him in the park are signs of adult responsibility, mothers and children. "The shadow of the playground fence was laid before me like a puzzle I had little chance of solving." Instead of pondering that puzzle, he buys an order of vegetable chow mein for Grandma Nettie, ribs for himself—

> Though I'd offer her a rib, I knew she wouldn't touch it and maybe not the chow mein even. Illness has a way of imposing its own orthodoxy. Yet I was determined to have her smiling, seeing her grandson eat, enjoying what I now believed to be one of her greatest pleasures.

"Spare Rib Park" is outrageous, and the self-absorbed narrator's image of life seems ready-made for the selfish, the greedy Americans of the Me-generation. Perhaps to know that, with plenty, we nevertheless live predatory lives would afford our times the means to fill the absence, the void modern life is. Steven Sher knows the absence, and he knows what is needed to fill it.

The nine stories here—some approaching brilliance and all fully-earned—arise from the artist's inner necessity to confront the enormity of our collective need. Unfortunately, a nation willing to believe that its hundreds of thousands of homeless people prefer the outdoors life is not likely to yield its belief that seeing us eat provides other people their greatest pleasure.

Leon V. Driskell
Louisville, 1989

MAN WITH A THOUSAND EYES
AND OTHER STORIES

BEASTS

Distracted, Schuyler looks up from his reading to watch a child run for the back of the bus, past the turning heads, with his mother in pursuit. Glancing out of the corner of an eye at the boy, perhaps three, he's reminded of a wild animal. He wonders how such a child belongs to this attractive woman: the child with a hairlip and large nose, flat as a fighter's, and crooked teeth. As their eyes meet and the boy smiles, Schuyler smiles back.

For all the sympathy he directs at the mother, she's silent and still, used to the attention. Having ignored the boy since they got on, she tries disowning him before the other passengers. Her hands fold in her lap as she stares blankly straight ahead. This enables her son to remain on his knees and look out the back of the bus, until he kicks her accidentally and she turns him around.

The boy's squirming feet reach just past the edge of the seat. That smile never stops, the magnet no one can resist, though when his mother looks, heads lower to their newspapers and paperbacks. Normal curiosity fails them. The boy remains playful, not questioning the silence.

After turning away any number of times, Schuyler finds himself caught and grinning unguardedly at the boy, receiving his twisted smile in return. Feeling the boy's eyes on him too long, he turns away, plotting the repair of that part of the face bent every-which-way.

By now, Schuyler's noticed no wedding band on the mother and how she's tried to smile, though hard for her, recognizing his bond with the boy. He nods at her and her look softens. Though all ears are turned in their direction, Schuyler decides to speak to her.

*

The boy's asleep in the bedroom in back and anything short of the roof's collapse, his mother warns, won't wake him. Shoeless, Schuyler is wine-high on the studio couch in the living room. He watches as she clears the dinette table, hears her stack the dishes in the sink.

Slowly spinning, the room is strangely bare. Life has passed without leaving much proof. A couple of crooked crayon drawings seem to float above the portable TV, across from the thriftshop couch. Schuyler can't guess what they're supposed to be. Cats, cut from a magazine, are taped to the same wall. A caricature of a child with oversized eyes hangs over the couch. There are no photographs of people anywhere in the apartment. Children's books, toy soldiers, a cereal box plane and a stuffed bear missing eyes have been pushed under the rocking chair or up against the one potted plant with few, huge leaves.

Schuyler lifts his head and stuffs a pillow behind it as he rolls from his back to his side, tucking his feet beneath the cushions at the end of the couch. He strains to put words to the TV picture. The volume is too low to hear.

Anita runs the water. His ears are drawn to the kitchen.

"Anything I can do to help?" he yells.

"I'm just going to let them soak."

The sound of the water changes, diminishes as the sink fills. She turns it off and steps into the dinette, blocking the light, bringing it in on her back and hair. Through wiping her hands, she hangs the dishtowel over the wicker back of a chair.

"The way you're sprawled out reminds me of his father."

"Is that good?"

"It's never done him any good."

Becoming absorbed in the program, she turns up the sound, moves Schuyler over with a look, and sits down on the edge of the couch. Both fix on the picture as if it's a face, motioning for them.

Schuyler's impulse is to stroke Anita, yet if he's clumsy about it, her laugh may be as disconcerting as the program's dubbed one. Lifting a hand to her back, he catches himself midway and lets it drop. He sits up pivoting to the edge of the couch, even with her, but it isn't enough to take her eyes off the TV.

"Why don't you let them operate on Barry? I've read they can do miracles with plastic surgery." He leans back on his hands, the arms locking, straight.

"I didn't ask for pity." She turns toward him, the light from the set on one side of her face. When she turns back to the show, Schuyler picks up one of his shoes and puts it on. The other is under the couch.

"Maybe I'll go for more wine." He finally shrugs, standing and tucking in his shirt where it's filled with air, and punches his arms through their jacket sleeves.

*

Sunday, on the way to the zoo, their silence intrudes on their good time. Schuyler, not used to the stares from passers-by, has let go of the boy's hand so they wouldn't associate the two of them in one thought. Birds are startled as the boy runs after them. Barry's eyes follow their flight, trying to keep up. Schuyler promises to buy him a helium balloon.

A vendor, first to smile at them all day, nods toward the boy, asking whether he'd like a frozen custard. Barry's eyes and ears are elsewhere, but Schuyler surprises him with a cone. Chocolate runs down his face and seems to set off rather than camouflage it.

Sensing people want to laugh at Barry as he licks his dripping mess, Schuyler barely holds onto his anger. When the boy finishes, his mother napkins his chin and cheeks, scrubbing hard, as if attempting to erase the features.

At the monkey house, they move directly to the front of the most crowded cage. The marmosets swing high, chasing moving tails. A sudden screech, stunning Barry, delights him.

"I like monkeys. I make monkey noise." He closes his eyes and screams, filling the monkey house, instigating more chatter from the cages.

"Only monkeys make monkey noise," says his mother. The smile is suddenly gone from his face. The eyes of people leaning into the railing are back on the monkeys.

One girl points at Barry and tugs at a man's sleeve. Schuyler can see the man's mouth moving, his eyes rolling back from Barry, explaining to the girl.

Barry takes Schuyler's hand tighter as he leads him to another cage where an orangutan slumps forward against the bars, reaching through for peanuts someone's thrown. It stuffs them into its mouth in lethargic sweeping motions. The boy pulls at the man's arm, leading him cage to cage.

Seeing that the two are getting on so well, Anita says she's tired and suggests they meet her at the cafeteria when they're through. Schuyler's actually glad to have her go. Barry's too busy watching the rhesus monkeys climb across their cage, clutching it as if they're pleading to be let out, to notice. The boy mouths the new monkey sounds he hears around him, testing them on his tongue, letting them slip soundlessly out.

Next and last is the cat house. The roaring almost stops the boy from going in, backed against Schuyler's leg, but Schuyler squats to explain that's how they tell the keeper they're hungry, or warn little boys if they've come too close.

The black leopard paces silently across its cage, repeating the same back and forth pattern. It turns toward the people behind the railing, catching their sight and scent. Barry pulls on his friend, aiming for the tiger cage where the keeper holds a hunk of raw meat. There are as many curious eyes on the boy as on the big cat tearing his dinner apart.

In the cafeteria, they spot Anita alone by a window. Barry's new balloon keeps bopping Schuyler's arm or chest as they move toward her.

"Did you have fun?" She looks up briefly as they take the seats across from her, then stares outside again. The leaves in front of the cafeteria are spread thick on the ground. Schuyler imagines her stare responsible for their abandoning the trees.

"Barry made friends with a tiger and a lion," he reports. Seeing the boy's difficulty trying to fit in the seat with the balloon, he ties the string to the back of the chair and centers the boy in it.

"Barry's right at home at the zoo." Schuyler looks up at her and decides she can't possibly mean that as it sounds. He digs inside his pocket for some change.

"I'll get drinks, if you think it won't interfere with his dinner," he offers. The boy insists on going too, provided his mother watches the balloon.

They head for the end of the line, studying the inside of the glass counter. Again she's staring in the direction of the trees and people laughing by the seals. Her head turns sharply when her son lets out a series of screams like those he's heard inside the monkey house.

*

What's left of dinner is turning cold out on the table. Barry's playing in the living room, distracted by the life-size stuffed monkey he's just received from Schuyler for his birthday. He's talking monkey talk to it. The adults are at the table, though Schuyler's eyes are cheating toward the boy. Barry pulls a party hat off his head and places it on the monkey, stretching the rubberband under the furry chin.

When Schuyler blows into a toy horn, the boy looks up and runs toward the table. He grabs it though his own is on the floor in the living room— but it somehow doesn't make the same strange, luring noise as Schuyler's. Giving it up, Schuyler sips on a beer.

At the incessant noise, Anita's face seems to crack a little more and finally, like something fragile giving way, it's had enough. Her anger breaks. She grabs for Barry's party favor. He dodges her, around the table.

"I think it's time you went to bed, young man. You've stayed up extra late for your birthday." She stands, waits and follows the boy, who pretends to fly into the bedroom after hugging Schuyler. The front of the apartment is suddenly quiet.

The man endures it better with his beer. He goes to the couch. Leaning back hard, missing the cushion, he bangs his head against the wall and laughs. He'd like to turn the TV on, but doesn't want to stand again; if there were only some way to think it into happening. So he stares at the blank set, conjuring a picture.

Soon he hears the woman enter. "Barry's gone to sleep." He turns from the TV and sees her sitting on the couch beside him.

"I have my own life. You don't know what I go through," she says. He grabs her by the arm, pulling her closer.

"Sometimes I think about giving him up for adoption."

"That's no way to talk."

"He loves you. He's never shown that to anyone before."

She leans against him. Allowing her head to stay on his chest, he strokes her hair. He feels the heat in her, that rapid breathing and her pulse that jumps the gap to him, receptive. His flesh is numb, unaware at first that she's on her feet and pulling on his hands, wanting him to stand.

She leads Schuyler to a chair in the dinette and sits him down. She removes the pillows from the studio couch, opens it into a bed and clicks the lamp down in the corner. The next thing he knows he's being tugged by the wrists across the room, then dropped suddenly on his back. Feeling her unzip his pants, he wonders how Barry feels when he has these things done for him. He closes his eyes. She touches him, flooding his mind. He makes low, grinning monkey noises.

"Shut up, beast," she says, covering his mouth.

*

Now when he takes off a day from work, Schuyler boards the bus swinging the child by his arms, knees tucked, up the front steps, then follows him all the way to the rear. If it's crowded, someone's always willing to get up and give the boy a seat. Inevitably, the person next to Barry also stands, giving Schuyler a seat too.

They're unaware to what extent they encourage overt eyes across the aisle, covert looks while someone's flipping to the next page in a book, wisecracks from high schoolers. Schuyler smiles through it all.

Sometimes they sit with their lunch bags in their

laps between their clasped hands— the man a perfect model— but when Barry gets up on his knees and looks out the window behind them, Schuyler follows his example.

"Barry, today I'll show you how to work the lions," announces Schuyler, and every head within range turns their way, all the ears waiting for more.

"Haven't you seen lion tamers before?" he asks a man standing close by, whose eyes have remained on Barry quite some time.

"I didn't mean to," blurts out the man, quickly retreating. The rows of heads turn back to books and newspapers, or to the sunny route that's now a blur.

The boy doesn't understand, but he laughs and busies himself again, playing a game with an imaginary toy. He flings his hands out of his lap into the air, as if brushing something up into the center of the bus. Tapping him on the arm, Schuyler puts his mouth to Barry's ear. He whispers, cupping his hands.

The two begin to giggle, but the other riders are distracted by that mob of teens, standing to leave, as they pound the glass and hurl themselves out the back exit. At the next stop, an incoherent bag lady won't step back from the door so the driver can close it. He refuses, despite her ranting, to let her on with all her bundles. The riders stare to hurry things along.

When that welcome quiet comes, Schuyler taps a twisty Barry on the knee. "Get ready." They place their hands around their mouths like megaphones. "Set." He pauses. "Now," he orders, and their monkey noises detonate across the moving bus, penetrating all the ears pretending to be deaf.

SPARE RIB PARK

When my grandparents stepped off the boat, they still kept kosher. Their household was established keeping strictly to the dietary laws—not even an unkosher word. Unless something was prepared in an Orthodox manner, my grandfather refused to eat. Not knowing what went on in a kitchen—even in a brother's home—was enough for him to consider its food *traif*. He mistrusted kosher claims and labels in English. He wondered whether meat and dairy plates were separately cleaned, whether food had been properly inspected, whether the prayer had been said. Even a rabbinical guarantee might have seemed insufficient proof. There were rabbis in America he didn't know.

So how's it that my grandmother, Nettie Eiseman, became more tolerant of the new ways? Maybe crossing to Brooklyn she tossed her excessive customs in the Atlantic, so she might set foot lighter on new land, with only the essentials. Maybe it takes a mother to accept change: better her children and her children's children should survive with the new than not at all.

"They don't bite," she assured me, my first time in a Chinese restaurant, while an entire plate of spare ribs cooled in front of us. I had pleaded to try them, having seen them eaten at another table occupied by neighborhood Jews. Sniffing, considering them, I slowly gained the courage to probe one with my fork.

"Doesn't your mother take you to eat out?" she asked. "You have to try things for yourself. Only then can you make decisions on what you base a lifetime."

"They don't look like anything she'd mind," I decided, trying to make it all right in case I overlooked an objection.

"It'll be our secret." She patted the air, as if that would ease my mind.

That she and her card players met one afternoon a week to eat chow mein, from the time this restaurant first appeared on the avenue, was already kept from my grandfather. Concessions for the grandchildren's sake were kept from him too: food unheard of in Europe, which Grandma Nettie served us off her kosher plates.

Honest to God, I didn't know what to do with the spare ribs until the waiter came by. Grandma's advising me with her hands hardly explained how to eat them, as if there were no equivalent translation. Letting them sit, at least to my mind, was nearly as good as koshering the meat.

When I finished the entire plate, I chewed around the bones where I might have missed something. Such a taste I couldn't imagine a crime to enjoy. Grandma Nettie seemed greatly pleased.

If she kept buying Chinese food, she might yet order spare ribs for herself one day. She might, in time, master the entire menu in Yiddish.

*

My Spare Rib Park is all cement except for a single sliding pond and row of swings, their chains often twisted in long braids, a sandbox and green creaking seesaws. Conveniently, the benches are in shadow, night or day, shaded by thick maples draping over the high fence. There are no lights where the uncurbed street dead ends. The weedy lots on the water side feed into the basin that will feed the larger bay.

On my bench I've carved my share of girls' initials. I always remember to carry my pocketknife on first dates, to impress them. We'll sit, my arm around a consenting shoulder, and watch the tall weeds sway about the basin's edge like silver blades set to attack. The moon gives everything away. I show off more than my wood artistry.

"It's too cold to be outside," my date might protest, after I've put her name into the wood. "I'm not in the mood."

"But it's good for you," I assure her, seeing her best color fill her cheeks, the challenge increased. "It improves the appetite."

Out beneath the open Brooklyn night a small boat might appear, motoring from the docks across the basin, drawing our attention to the necklace-stretch of bright street lights, shoreline traffic. As if we've conspired with the night against it, the moon, so much like my grandfather's stern face, will seem to turn away from us. We go ahead with the spare ribs anyway.

Quite the nose-teaser, the smell of Chinese food makes me forget our laws forbidding it, also the cold and, at times, my date. I choose thin, bustless types— not an extra ounce of anything, unlike the meatier spare ribs that I prefer— the kind I can bring home for my mother to fatten up, girls with unmistakable faces and cavernous appetites.

Our neighborhood's original Chinese restaurant still attracts customers like a magnet off the main avenue. Its manager, the only Oriental without a white jacket and bowtie, keeps his greeting simple. His eyes close into thin slits. His mouth widens. Like a puppet he shakes his head to his energetic smile.

"The spare rib boy, yes? Order for two?" He watches for my date's reaction, folding his hands in his chest.

"Could you throw in extra duck sauce?" I beg him, clearing for the taste with several huge swallows.

"Good customer," he tells my date.

Before he heads for the kitchen, he'll place a bag of noodles on the glass display case, so we might take the edge off our hunger. If he's seen the girl more than a few weekends in a row, he'll leave fortune cookies instead.

While the order is prepared, I'm careful not to let my date stray too close to the tables, as she might want to get off her feet right then and there.

We leave and walk toward the park. The bag swings in my hand to quicken us, marking the pace against my thigh. Sometimes, depending how close she walks, how tightly she holds on, I give a preview of the ribs. Opening the top of the bag, a proud parent showing off the baby in the carriage, I instruct her to put her nose to it, breathe deeply. The reserve is taken out of her.

"Tell me these aren't the best ribs you've ever

smelled?" I ask, and it seems I'm comparing myself to other boys.

There's a great silence. I'm not so sure how she's taken anything I've said, but the ribs now demand undivided attention, like ritual observance, over all else.

We enter the park. Napkins are spread out in our laps. The insulated bag, torn open, is set upon the bench beside us. All prerequisites concluded, I prepare to unkosher her.

*

Some weeks friends call—begging sometimes—to borrow my park. Some even offer to set me up for the night if I okay their horning in on my prime territory.

"If you need money, you'll be taken care of. You have my word."

"It's nothing to do with money."

"Ribs are on me."

"I don't know. There's more to it."

Another's distraught because his date is tentative at best unless he comes up with acceptable plans, and it's already mid-week.

"If you're not going to be busy..."

"Not busy on a Saturday night?" I'm hurt by such an accusation, hoping it won't get around. "Are you for real?"

"We can double then. Maybe catch a movie and afterward wind up in opposite corners of the park. What do you say?" he might persist.

"You can do the same things after you take her home."

"Her parents wait up. They won't let us out of their sight."

Then there are those friends who won't warn me at all. I might find one on my bench working his date over in the dark, the two passionately embraced. I'll smell their spare ribs, the aphrodisiac that starts a couple off. His technique will stir my date's suspicious mind.

Can there be more than one spare rib operator? she'll wonder. I'll pretend not to know the guy already winning his date over with all my tested methods. Can there be a whole gang of spare rib fanatics? I'll anticipate this line of thinking, suffering right then for my success.

The night might come when all bench space is taken and the pocketknives, pulled out at once, compete for the remaining wood. There's no telling how far it'll go. Some wiseguy might spray paint over my carved log of names. Another might violate my dictum of spare ribs by bringing something other than Chinese. Here such a choice wouldn't be kosher. This park has its own customs to uphold.

*

Before Grandma Nettie became ill, I brought her to see my park so she might have an idea what dating had come to since her time. Having heard about my generation, interested in anything I did, she was determined that I take her there. Finally I agreed, so long as it was during the day.

We stopped at the Chinese restaurant first. I ordered spare ribs at her suggestion, while she decided on her usual vegetable chow mein. Although she paid for everything, she let herself be led to the park as willingly as a schoolgirl.

"So this is where you take your girlfriends?" she asked, when we reached my bench and I helped her sit, one hand under her arm.

Grandma Nettie leaned back cautiously against the cuttings in the wood. I could see her face ask: Who would do such a thing? So I kept the answer to myself. She offered me half of her container of chow mein. Before I could make up my mind, she shoveled it onto the insulated bag opened in my lap.

"We come here after the date, grandma. It's a chance to be alone before I take a girl home."

Without looking, she scooped a spoonful of chow mein from the bottom of the container. Her face withdrew fast, eyes tearing. She held the food in her mouth, too hot still to swallow. Stirring what remained, she blew into it and it steamed into the air. She waited before taking another bite cautiously in her front teeth.

"Girls these days expect to be fed," I continued.

"You've got to make a date think you're someone special." I offered her a rib, but she refused as always, gesturing for me to enjoy them all.

"You find yourself a nice girl and she'll think you're special without the Chinese food. Don't they like necking anymore?" she asked. This time she was careful to blow on her food before setting it on her tongue.

I shrugged my shoulders, embarrassed. "It's just that one without the other isn't enough."

"We didn't know from chow mein," she assured me. "Thank God your grandfather doesn't know. It's meant for your generation. American tastes are different."

She leaned back heavily against the carvings in the bench. Her cane was hooked onto the top slat, at her side. Her smile seemed to approve of my tactics with the girls. Spare ribs weren't enough to get me in trouble.

"Are your girlfriends Jewish?" she asked, still chewing. Swallowing went easier now that her chow mein was cooling. "You know your parents have the highest hopes for you."

I stared at my last rib but couldn't pick it up. My parents probably didn't mind spare ribs, but would've been infinitely happier if I didn't enjoy them quite so much. The same was true for girls.

"I still have kosher tastes in girls, grandma. The rest is only food."

I began on my spare rib before something else would keep me from it. After squeezing a line of duck sauce from its packet, I licked my fingertips of grease. Bones, cleaned nearly white, were all that was left in my lap.

When, the next time, I went back, I carved her initials twice as large as all the rest because the park now felt as comfortable as my grandmother's house. "May you live and be well, Grandma Nettie," I heard myself saying, "and enjoy your great grandchildren someday."

But as God would have it, within a few months doctors discovered spreading cancer. Although she still looked like her old self, they rushed her suddenly to the hospital, where she came under supervision stricter than maintaining kosher.

From the start, my mother visited the hospital every day, at the same stroke of the same hour, so Nettie wouldn't worry something happened. As for grandma, she wore the same expression so her daughter wouldn't worry that her condition was worse. Even a smile at the wrong time could be seen as an attempt to hide something, to cover up a loved one's pain.

Our family has a long history of not being able to hide anything from the women. To this day when something bothers me, even if I don't realize it shows, my mother knows, simply by an intuition so refined, mother to daughter, that it takes the guesswork out of emotion. If I refuse something I like at dinner, I'm presumed sick, though I might've grabbed a quick snack half an hour before. If I don't go out on Saturday night, call the family doctor. If I refuse to eat spare ribs, I'm definitely ill beyond words and worry.

So when my parents asked me to accompany them to the hospital, I said no as often as yes. Knowing how much I cared for grandma, they must have suspected I was sick to my soul to turn down any chance to see her and cheer her up. Actually, I was unsure whether cheering up was what Nettie needed in her condition. Maybe worry instead, like my mother's, was the proper remedy. As it was, I visited when I felt up to it and could handle seeing her double-teamed by age and sickness. Hospitals, unlike Chinese food, were not an easily acquired taste.

For the first time, I began going to my Spare Rib Park during the day to think alone. Sometimes I'd sit for hours—until finally located by a messenger of worry sent by the family—whittling at the bench or watching small boats stir in the basin, adding animation to a world that had temporarily lost its color and its movement. Pain worked deeper on my face. Such a retreat on a Saturday night would bring me nothing but an early request home.

*

While my grandmother was undergoing many

tests and subsequent surgery, I began to see one steady girl. The park became her park as well as mine, though I never admitted to anyone that it was really Grandma Nettie's. I knew she'd probably just as soon give it away as anything that might be hers, seeing how we children enjoyed it.

"Don't you ever get tired of spare ribs and this dumb park?" my girl asked me one night, after we had leaned against her initials for a month of Saturdays. "You're just interested in one thing. You're no more romantic than any other guy."

Locking her arms in her chest, she set her back up like a barricade. I stood and shook her shoulders to turn her around. The face was no longer familiar. What happiness would be mine if I could find a face as pretty— so long as it was kind.

"At least," she went on, "the others are blunt about what they want. No pretending under the stars and moon. No eating out of a bag. They make tables so people don't have to eat out of laps. And plates so we don't have to eat off paper."

"You know what your problem is?" I blurted out, moving her back when my hand slapped a boundary in the air between us— preparing it for my words— daring her to step across. But I couldn't think of anything to say.

With great effort I avoided her face. It had so easily turned my head before. Now we sat independently on far sides of the bench, as if it were a seesaw evenly balanced. Stubbornly I faced the basin, concentrating on the boats and lights.

My thoughts found words, having wrestled them down. "You make excuses you're bored because you've gotten too close."

"Egomaniac. Who can get close to someone with meat between his teeth? Your kisses are as greasy as your spare ribs."

I pushed away from where we inadvertently touched, two occupying forces at that point of contact. It was more unbearable than sitting through a double feature with an arm around her shoulder.

When I turned to face her again, she was up and

walking off, so being a gentleman I followed her to make sure that she arrived home safely. Once she got there, she slammed the door without giving me a chance to do more damage to her feelings. It would've been better had I tried to cop a little something, at least giving her legitimate reason to be sore. Another girl was already on reserve. It would be a simple matter to ask her for a date. Impatiently, I began to visualize her face. I'd picture it all week until, blown out of proportion, it would become an overwhelming distraction from the difficulty of these days.

First, on our big night, I'd make sure how she felt about Chinese. Then I might introduce her to my Spare Rib park— something she wouldn't expect nor be prepared for on a first date. It would be like bringing her home. Lights around the basin would impress her. I'd initiate her with an unkosher kiss, from sticky ribs. Then I'd promise to carve her initials in the bench next to grandma's, maybe as large. An empty space, once found, would be prepared. Those most recent initials, a name I wouldn't dare repeat, were already scratched out of my mind.

*

As if the weekend weren't already depressing enough, Sunday had been promised to the family for visiting the hospital. While I was willing to give my Sunday up for Grandma Nettie, I knew she'd never ask me to give up anything for her. She was convinced that my youth, even if it meant her sacrificing something, deserved every chance. If only I could find a girl who would be satisfied so easily, not even spare ribs would be necessary. My appetite would be satisfied for all time, for all nights, without the words and kisses that promised more than someone eventually gave.

Having finished breakfast, I was out of the house unannounced a good while before the family hoped to leave. I walked quickly, my hands stuffed inside my pockets, hoping to slow the spread of worry. I fought to keep a lid on how I felt.

Once inside the park I claimed my bench. I

thought about girls for awhile, expecting it would take the bad edge off how I felt. But the location was too recently spoiled: *Imagine her, walking out on me.* I spit into the wind. She was probably waiting by the phone and would jump at my offer of spare ribs.

I could see the houses on the opposite shore lined above the docks and ramps. Boats bobbed up against brick. Sun rippled the water's mirrored surface. I became distracted by children running through the park to join others on the swings and sliding pond where they went headfirst down. The shadow of the playground fence was laid out before me like a puzzle I had little chance of solving. Young mothers pushed their baby carriages into the shade. One led her first-walking child away from the sandbox. His fingers were wet with sand and he cried when she slapped it off his palms.

I got up from my bench and turned to leave. My family would begin to wonder where I disappeared to—the worry brigade dispatched.

For Grandma Nettie, thinking it might cheer her up, I bought an order of vegetable chow mein to go, and ribs for me, from the Chinese restaurant with what was left of my date money. Packed in their insulated bags, they would stay hot until I snuck them past the nurses into grandma's room. Though I'd offer her a rib, I knew she wouldn't touch it and maybe not the chow mein even. Illness has a way of imposing its own orthodoxy. Yet I was determined to have her smiling, seeing her grandson eat, enjoying what I now believed to be one of her greatest pleasures.

LOVERS

The day Mrs. Schumacher died, her friends in the Skyview Nursing Home came apart at their raggedy seams. It wasn't death so much, expected in such a place at any time, but jealousy that they too couldn't leave. Like elephants staggering to the burial grounds, they were stuck and sinking slowly with the weight of burdensome age and pain.

While others mourned, Molly Perlman felt much better than she had in months, having received new glasses for her "cadillac" so she could see again, though not yet clearly, out of her corrected eye.

She forced her walker to the elevator past her neighbors who never left their rooms or were dropped off in wheelchairs in front of the communal television. She needed to get away from the third floor. Already that morning she had misplaced her old glasses. Her one unbroken tube of lipstick had been missing since breakfast, a pill bottle of saccharin brought back in its place. That pair of stockings she had hung in the bathroom to dry was gone as well.

The large gameroom buzzed with the only facsimile of life in the entire seven floors. Max, inviting new rumors, was waiting where every day he met her after breakfast. But talk of Mrs. Schumacher predominated, with Skyview residents pitching themselves in the direction of death rather than speculating about the lovers.

"I see you got your glasses today," Max said, measuring her distance from the couch and the time she took to reach it. Looking into the sun in one of the gameroom picture windows, Molly got turned around trying to locate his voice.

"It's amazing what they can do," she said, once seated, fixing the glasses on her nose. He took her obedient hands into his lap and held them. "Except a lot of good it did Mrs. Schumacher."

"It's like horses. One day they put you out to

pasture." With his cane he slapped his thigh above his replacement and sat erect on the edge of the couch. "Better they shoot me and end it all."

"What kind of talk is that from a man in good health other than missing a leg?" She swung around to face him, searching for an opening in his face.

Hesitating, he looked into his lap at their hands, clasped like schoolchildren's. "For someone your age, Molly..."

"And what's wrong with my age? You're not so far from it, Mr. Sarnoff."

"Forgive me," he said, and it seemed he was apologizing before all the busybodies squinting at them across the gameroom. Then he spat out "We should get married, Molly," like a bad taste in his mouth he had picked up from this place.

Molly considered what he said as if she were deciding what to have for dinner, boiled chicken or chipped beef. "You don't want me." She batted the air with her laugh.

"I'm no longer independent," she continued. Her thoughts, like hot stones, were lobbed across the couch for him to catch. "What do you want with a treestump that will soon be cleared away?"

"Haven't you been a widow going on twenty years? Aren't you curious anymore?" He adjusted his glasses, raising his eyes.

"Max, you overestimate me. I'm held together by medicine, held up by this walker. Let's keep our respect for each other."

She raised a knotted hand and ran it through her hair. Once like steel wool, it was now straight and thinning like a doll's. He squeezed her hand and pulled it back into his lap.

"I know everything I need to know about you," he admitted, as if the matter were decided. Her eyes, widening, seemed to fill the frames of her new glasses.

"If I make plans, I'd like to keep them," reasoned Molly, considering the years she had lived alone. "If I say no, the whole building will find out and it'll be hard on you. But if I say yes, they may let us leave. What choice do you give me?"

He nodded there was none as his eyes settled on the large screen across the way, past a blind spot the direct sun made, where the loud game show competed with the talk about Mrs. Schumacher.

*

Jack Perlman would always visualize his mother in these, her fading years, when he couldn't help but notice the rapid ravages of time. Week after week he came out of respect to see her. To pass the hour, he told jokes she probably didn't hear. He filled her in on the world as if she'd been transported to a far-off place, a different time, and she became nostalgic. He dared not mention her apartment had been rented to someone else. Hoping she'd hear what was impossible—Jack finally telling her she could go home—Molly contented herself with these brief visits, pretending she was still the matriarch though all her children had built lives without her.

This dedicated son, who never seemed to mind how she was always building up his brothers and sisters, made excuses when they stayed away: telling her that Murray was making lots of money in his new career; reminding her that Katie had moved to Arizona for her arthritis years before and that Rose came when the kids allowed; lying about Bernie, her favorite, still teaching in California, when in fact he had died of cancer the year before. Jack, sitting *shive*, came to visit his mother with a forced smile and the usual jokes, afraid to risk the shock of that bad news.

"A lovely son, Mrs. Perlman," Mrs. Schumacher used to say, waiting for her own family to arrive. "Is he an actor or something?"

"One week he brings me stockings, chocolate bars the next. Would another son remember?" Molly would sigh. The memory of her other sons was fading, like old photographs.

On his first visit after her cataract operation, Jack was taken back by how old, bolstered up in bed, his mother looked. Her face seemed then to have gained a line for every day at Skyview, lost a shade of color. The name bracelet gapped on her wrist and her bosom sagged beneath her bedclothes—fruit rotted on the vine. Uncovered, one ankle swelled thigh-width, skin smooth as glaze. Convinced she was failing fast, he flinched from that change he felt most deeply, his mother's bandaged eye. He had looked into her eyes all his life, possibly missing their significance.

It was a different Molly when he visited after she had recovered and was wearing her thick glasses. She seemed fit but distant, like a fly or bee seen under magnification.

"I may not be a Perlman for long," she said, breaking their silence. She allowed him his startled look. "It's not what you're thinking. Max asked me to marry him. I said yes, but I want your opinion first."

"You mean Max with the leg?" He raised an arm and shook his fist, threatening as Max did with his cane.

"Maybe you can fix up my apartment," she continued, ignoring his remark. "It'll be nice to have someone to share it."

Fearing she'd suspect the truth about her apartment if he allowed her to pursue it, Jack instead went on at length about the prospects of marriage at her age. Molly pressed him for his answer.

"What about children, mother?"

"Be serious a moment."

"Have you thought of simply living in sin?"

When visiting time ended, the son automatically stood and helped his mother rise. As he escorted her to the third floor so she could prepare for dinner, he still kidded her about his having another brother or a sister at her age. She took the kidding to mean he approved of her plan. Though who could ever really tell with him?

*

Whenever Max's daughter visited, it was as much to see her as Max, thought Molly, and always with a gift: lipstick or some magazine, maybe a knish or bagel from the avenue, though Molly at the latter always shook her head, thanked Lilly anyway, and explained how some things were impossible to eat without the teeth for it. A girl like this was to Max's credit.

On the day Max broke the news about the wedding, he led his daughter across the gameroom toward his intended bride. Lost in the whirl of activity around her, Molly tried to read their approaching faces. When they reached her, she was nonchalantly chatting with a woman on the next couch, each gesturing as if the other were halfway across the room.

Lilly sat and took her hand, finding Molly's pulse, gently. "Dad's told me the good news. Of course I couldn't be happier." After hugging her, she handed the prospective bride a paper bag with a staple where the cashier's slip had been ripped off.

"You always bring such nice things. You treat me better than my own," said Molly, allowing Lilly to unfold the scarf and hold it up beside her face so they could get an idea how it would look. Max shook his head agreeably, feigning interest, his ears on the television.

"Children leave home. They forget," decided Molly.

"Whose are any better?" asked Lilly. "It depends on your situation and your luck."

"Then you don't mind if I think of you as a daughter?"

"If it's how you feel."

"My daughters never come to visit, and of the boys only one ever shows up."

"Jack's a regular," intercepted Max.

Molly, annoyed at his butting in, gave him a look to shut him up and then continued. "Is keeping an old lady company once in awhile asking so much?" she asked, shrugging her shoulders. "Without family they might as well shovel the dirt over you."

"Come to the point, Molly," Max insisted, spreading his hands, encouraging her.

"I have a daughter who's never been here and a son whose face I've forgotten. Since you're almost a daughter...," she paused, tucking in her lower lip, "...Max and I were wondering whether you'd put us up until my apartment's ready."

"You wouldn't want newlyweds to stay in a place

like this, would you?" asked Max.

"There's not much I can do," said his daughter, shifting uneasily, leaning back out of range of the hope set in their eyes. They tried to read her expression as if their life together depended on it. "I have a family of my own and barely enough room for them."

"We wouldn't stay too long," said Molly.

"Where else would you get this kind of care?" Lilly looked past them, her eyes wandering from television to couch to a blur of animation about the room.

"Why can't we?" pressed Max. "What's important is that Molly and I get out of here now. It's impossible to live like a person."

"I don't know what my father's told you," Lilly said, turning to the older woman. "When he lived in our finished basement after his last wife died, he complained plenty— about missing friends, about the cold and how there were no windows. But there's no room down there now."

Molly choked on the words which stuck like bones in her throat: "last wife"— *How many altogether?* For the rest of the visit, she sat as inconspicuously as with her own children, inwardly suffering. She could have been polite if prompted, though it would have brought her into the conversation against her will. But Max avoided her eyes brewing darker, too strong to take, beneath Molly's thick glasses that had cut the couple off.

*

By morning, Molly had confined herself to bed without explanation. The doctor found nothing wrong, but even with all his convincing she remained silent. Other patients were wheeled past her open door into breakfast, like a shipment of headstones, all with the same blank faces and eyes.

An aide came in with breakfast, opened the curtains and turned Molly from her side onto her back. The early sunlight through her window made her squint, but by midday it had shifted and the room again was draped with shadow. She refused to get up or explain and her pretending became easier the longer she lay in bed, refusing to respond to shaking and encouragement alike. She offered no resistance except gravity. Her appetite went. Each shift of light and dark across her room seemed like a change of bandages.

On the second day after breakfast, Max finally paid the visit she'd been waiting for. He called to her before approaching. With her back to the doorway, moaning so he could hear, she disguised her voice as if in pain and bid him come in. For several moments he stood over her, facing the warm sunlight through the window. Her situation registered and turned his head her way.

Max pulled up a chair, scraping linoleum, and hung his cane on the bed's metal bars once seated.

"How do you feel?" He aimed for the ear that wasn't against the pillow, choosing the leverage he believed would get her up. "I was worried when you didn't show up. I heard you were sick, so I decided to see for myself."

Though she didn't move, he sensed her open eyes, that she had heard him. "Everyone asks about you. Of course I tell them it's only a temporary setback. That Molly Perlman and I are engaged."

Having plotted her move, Molly shifted onto her back like a turtle turning its shell. Her eyes strayed across the room, passing over her roommate's empty bed before centering on Max. She could only make out his blurred shape, but knew that persuasive voice too well.

She pointed to the dresser next to her bed. "My glasses. Hand me my glasses." He put them in her hand and closed it around them.

"What could you possibly have to say for yourself, Mr. Sarnoff?" she started, hoisting herself higher on the pillows. "The engagement is off. Leave this old body in peace."

"The other day you were telling my Lilly that she was like a daughter to you."

"How many mothers can a girl have? How many women have you brought home for her blessings?"

"Don't talk foolish. We've both led full lives, but

they're not over," he insisted, folding his arms in his chest.

"At least my Sam, may he rest in peace, was sincere. No gigolo like some men."

"You're no virgin yourself, Molly."

Shaking him off, she turned back onto her side, using the bed's metal bar for support. She closed her eyes to avoid the light pushing deeper into the room.

"You should be ashamed, leading someone on like that," she said, raising her voice, coughing. Heads peeked in from the hallway, one shaking violently as if to free itself from some awful hold. They were ready to pay their respects at a moment's notice.

"I could've had my pick. No shortage of willing women here," muttered Max.

"Falling for your tricks— at my age." Molly stretched her open arms toward the ceiling. "Mrs. Schumacher, you at least went in peace. Have them start shoveling."

"If that's all you have to say, I'll be going." He stood, unbending slowly, as if considering the distance to the door. "If you change your mind, you'll find me at the usual place."

More residents had gathered in the doorway, but Max scattered them like birds as he hobbled into the hall, grumbling past the aide who rushed to the room when she saw the crowd.

*

When Jack came that weekend and found his mother in the gameroom on the roof, it was not the same woman he had recently visited. She followed him intently as he stepped from the elevator— long before the elevator door opened, she had watched— and approached her corner of the room. The distractions of the crowded visiting hour were of no consequence to her. At last, her Jack.

He couldn't recall the last time she had worn make-up, a pale lipstick, powder and rouge, or that flowered dress, now terribly wrinkled, she had worn into the nursing home, unprepared for what she'd find, unwilling to stay. Seeing her this way reminded him of the arguments she used to give him. Her one concession to comfort was the pair of open-toe slippers she normally wore for her swollen feet. Something definitely was up, but still Jack wasn't expecting the reception he received.

"Take me home today or I'll walk out on my own."

She began to stand, but his leaning over to kiss her kept her seated. Her brief fast from life had exposed her to eternity and it was enough: not another day to be wasted, here.

When he mentioned Max's name, there was a cough from her and a wince of recognition. Believing she would try to leave and wind up hurting herself, Jack told her that her apartment had been let go, seeing as she gave him no choice, and there was nothing they could do about it. Although she had guessed at this truth long ago, his saying it made it seem final only now.

"Another son wouldn't let them keep me prisoner," she said, harping on a theme he had heard before, hoping he'd offer a way out. But as he dismissed each plea, her resistance decreased. She slumped back in her seat in silence.

Then the visit was over before she knew it. Jack helped her stand and saw her down to the third floor before she told him she'd go on alone, seeing his elevator off.

The way Molly felt, it seemed more a matter of inevitability than convenience when she sat to think in front of the television in the lobby on her floor, joining those who bobbed their heads like marionettes or slept to the overamplified blur. Her more capable eyes circled them; confined to their wheelchairs and seats, they couldn't leave. How she envied their ebbing lives, these lucky ones, each more deserving than she to follow Mrs. Schumacher.

PIGEON SOUP

As was her custom in the coolness of the morning, deaf to the rattling el above and the humming avenue, Rose strolled, unusually light-footed, among strangers, the smell of food being prepared and the ocean air engaging her. The shopping bag she carried was empty now, but on a good day she'd return to her walk-up clutching dinner's main course, though it might take her most of the morning to catch.

Stopping outside the shops, she rested every block to examine the curious fish on ice, the rows of holiday cakes and rolls, loaves of braided challah. Fresh crates, fruits and vegetables, displays of borscht and imported dates neatly stacked beside blocks of halvah lit her memory. A group of schoolchildren eyeing candy, gathering outside a luncheonette, forced her to swing wide on the sidewalk. It was just as well. Looking was for those who came to spend.

She shuffled along, following her usual route, caught her face in plateglass once and wondered whether she'd be lucky. She had learned over the years to live with little, but her tabby boarder needed to build back its strength. Unable to fend for itself, underweight and badly gashed when it appeared at Rose's window a few months before, the cat securely curled in the woman's narrow lap from that first day on. So Rose looked after it as if it were a child, now grown, returning home.

The long blocks at her slow pace firmed her resolve. She saw her first pigeons of the day, but the street was walled here with delivery trucks, making the birds nervous. One quick flutter and they all took acrobatically to the air.

Nearing the park, Rose saw them cluster. A car honked and they jumped from the corner. When someone late for work went running by to catch the train, they scattered to the trees. Taunted by hunger, they soon swooped down again.

She found a bench a short distance from the scavenging flock. One bony hand went deep inside her shopping bag. Systematically, she scattered seed in the birds' direction, giving them a trail to chase, then sprinkled some between her feet. She sat back and waited. Sunlight filled her face, a harmless mask atop her statue's pose.

Young running children chased the pigeons from the path. But the birds, not to be deterred, returned to feed. A businessman passed, swinging his briefcase. The flock backed off in a nervous strut, their heads bobbing like corks on water.

When again the birds forgot their fear, they ate their way to the woman's bench. Cooing loudly, the fatter, greedier ones came daringly close to Rose's feet. Lulled by their own cooing, it seemed, and insatiable appetites, they dipped their beaks, then shook the seed down.

She pounced cat-like upon the closest, fattest pigeon of them all, took it tightly by the neck and snapped the life from it. Cooing urgently, the others flapped to flight above the street, to the safe tenements and el. They perched like judge and jury over Brighton.

She breathed hard now, exhilarated, snorting the feathered air where the brief struggle took place. What a fine catch, she thought, quickly collecting her things, and took the shortest path out of the park, past the spooked birds. Her eyes never strayed from pavement as she swung the weighted bag from her thin wrist. The first drops of blood showed on the bottom of the bag, soaking fast. She hurried to get off the street.

*

Before Rosh Hashanah, Rose took the lone box with her best dress down from her closet and put it on. It hadn't been worn for a year or washed in God-knew-how-many, and the red camellia pattern was grease-stained and creased. She remembered when the dress was new and she wore it for her family. There must have been good times, she guessed, but now she had to dig below the rough years to retrieve them.

It was hard enough remembering the recent months. All Rose recalled was taking in the injured cat, then growing weak herself for all her caring for a living thing again. In gratitude, the cat had killed a sparrow on the fire escape and carried it in its mouth to Rose's chair. They shared that catch; the woman's cooking it to repay the cat's kindness irrevocably spoiled the pet so it never caught another meal.

Now as she returned to her apartment to ready for the holiday, Rose noticed something different about her permanent guest. Its usual soft-footed bounce from the windowsill was clumsy and its belly hung low. *Of course.* It had in recent days stayed close to the open window, lacking its usual curiosity. *How could I have missed the signs?*

She sighed without showing her true disappointment. "What's to come won't be easy." She stroked the cat, feeling its belly for the pink nipples that had sprouted as quickly as potato eyes.

Sniffing at the shopping bag beside the stove, the cat pawed for the day's catch. Rose obediently cut off the pigeon's head and tossed it to the cat, then cleaned and put the rest whole in the soup. When the bird had cooked enough to flavor the broth, she gave it all to her pet.

Hoping to catch another meal, she lined the shopping bag with clean newspaper, then wrapped her shawl around her shoulders. The full cat sprawled out, sagging on the kitchen floor, eyes sealed, mouth hanging open. Only its nose seemed to be working, sniffing the soupy air the way it might dislodge a fly.

Rose was quickly down the dim five flights, out on the busy street among the faces that in passing made her happy this time of the year. She worried that the birth would come without warning, at any time.

Toward dusk, as the holiday called the men away to pray, she returned with another pigeon in her bag. Its eyes, as she laid it out across the kitchen counter, remained open, still suspicious. Enticing this one hadn't been so easy. Trapping it had taken most of what was left of Rose's seed.

She packed the dead bird in the fridge, knowing

it would soon be gone judging from the way the cat had torn at the day's first meat, deboning the cooked flesh, dragging it off the plate onto the floor. The mother-to-be sprawled lazily on the fire escape.

Rose poured herself clear soup and sat at the open window over the alley where darkness pooled, rising higher against the tenement backs. Out of sight the street still pulsed with life. She let her bowl of steaming soup cool. Her hands, tired and bloody, wrapped around it without feeling.

Dreamily, she shuddered from the chill that had slipped inside. Her apartment was dark except for the low flame still under the soup, the reflection of the restless cat's eyes and an electric clock on the table.

Not thinking to turn on a light, which might have let her see the confinement she already felt, she relived the fleeting images her apartment harbored, a conscience that would ease with light. The darkness tested Rose's threadbare hope. She located the cat again by the sound of crunching bone. Suddenly, leaping into Rose's lap, it was complaining to be fed. Her eyes shut for the sadness they saw ahead.

*

On the eve of Yom Kippur, as Brighton peaked with solemn celebration, tremors of atonement shook the courtyards. Rose was sure this brought on labor. Before the evening services were done, her cat gave birth to a litter of four under the open window in her small apartment.

Seeing the cat stretch limp, licking its litter, Rose wondered how long the mother could nurse without nourishment herself. As many pigeons as Rose brought home the last ten days, the cat ate. But the seed was gone. As it had diminished, her quick hands became impatient traps. The pigeons knew to keep their distance. The meals decreased. Now, after the quart of milk she bought with her last bit of change, there was nothing left to feed the cat, and no relief in sight until her check arrived.

She poured herself clear soup for dinner before her day-long fast, but felt guilty for even that when the mother cat sniffed at the serving in its bowl and wouldn't eat. Answering those first uncertain cries of life, the mother nursed as long as she could, then stood and leaped onto the windowsill. When the mewing renewed and got to be too much for her, she slipped out onto the fire escape beyond the immediate range of their demands.

"It's forbidden to eat, but you're an exception. A mother's got to nurse." The cat returned halfheartedly to lick the huddle of fur that tried to wobble to its feet on the newspaper spread over the floor. "I'll borrow food tomorrow," the woman swore.

Rose in her chair by the window slept in spurts, forgetting to turn off the gas under the soup, so that the liquid boiled down, burnt solid on the bottom. She tried to arrive at reasons for the bad luck of the last few days. She had gone without food before, but new life couldn't live on promises. Mother cat, responding to that piercing of the dark, paced between the fire escape and her kittens when they woke.

Before first light the woman left, hooking the shopping bag over her wrist, her shawl pulled taut. She took each landing slowly, trying to remember neighbors on each floor, but she'd had no contact with them for so long, no one except unfamiliar tenants who never spoke.

Next to the building, she found a better shopping bag out with the trash and lined it with clean newspaper. With this omen, she imagined that her luck was meant to turn. Her old bag, smeared with feathers and with blood, was wearing through the bottom.

Summoning courage, she entered a cheese and meat store owned by gentiles, just opening for the day, and asked if they could spare some scraps. The owner laughed and pointed to the fat tom behind the counter. At the few shops open on the avenue, she heard the same. Trying a supermarket beyond the predominantly Jewish blocks, she explained her situation once again. The busy grocer shook his head and moved past her to his paying customers. Discouraged, she considered stealing what she needed, here where they didn't know her. Maybe she could give away the kittens on the street. But they were much too young to separate from their mother.

When Rose returned midday, her body ached from her trying pace since daybreak. The difficult hours had disguised her face. Climbing the long flights of stairs empty-handed, she let go of her thoughts, struck numb.

She fell into a chair, ankles swollen. Begging for food, the cat began to rub against her legs. Soon she was able to spoon a bowl of cold soup from what had boiled down and stuck. When she set out the bowl, the new mother meowed and ran to the dish, but wouldn't eat the paste, instead complaining. The kittens now cried louder, as if someone had turned up the sound while Rose was gone.

As afternoon sealed off the tenement, the litter became more frantic the more their mother ignored them. Unable to nurse them anymore, the cat leaped to the fire escape and turned away. Pacing, she looked back again, fighting to control her instincts.

"It would be much better for them had you remained an alley cat," the old woman said, covered by shadow. "By now you've forgotten how to hunt for food."

There was no shutting them up. Rose's nervous pet was in her lap one moment and out the next to comfort her young or leap onto the windowsill to stare. All sense of time was lost. The outside light no longer reached them, dusk having dropped down the deep well of tenements placed back to back.

"Soon you'll be sucked to nothing but ribs. If only I could be your wet-nurse," offered Rose, "but I'm too old."

As she stood and changed out of her red camellia dress, she summoned snatches of the *Kaddish* she had said over her family long ago. She was moved to place the screaming, twisting litter one by one into the soft material, then lowered them into the shopping bag hung on her wrist.

She was afraid her walking through the streets would attract attention at this hour, expecting the holiday throng to break, a sudden animation that would offset the city's stillness, stingy light. Past gated stores, the traffic just a trickle down the avenue, she felt her heart support a weary weight that moved without food or sleep, holding no hope for what she was about to do.

Rocked by the slow walk, the kittens' muffled cries increased. They were too hungry to sleep. Rose avoided looking at them though she felt their insignificant weight, the way a pigeon might feel on another day.

She walked along the esplanade until she came to where it seemed the rocks were hurled ashore by storms. Placing the bundle upon the crumbling sea wall, she took out the dress and wound it tightly around the fighting life within. She ignored the pleas, closing her eyes.

Lifting them above her head, she held them there, weighing the situation one more time. Then, as if a hand were guiding her, she dumped the bundle in the water. A frightened gull, at the splash, took off from broken piling. The ocean rippled as it moved in, like an open hand accepting gifts. Soon the camellias took in too much water and the cloth, caught in the closing fist, began to sink.

MAN WITH A THOUSAND EYES

For most of three-quarters of a century, Goldstein has spoken alarmingly of death, seeing the years come faster as he moves more slowly through them toward life's lean side. "I don't believe in miracles," he says, "except I always seem to make it to another day." Still his eyes, seeing all, are dry and clear, his mind filled with stories to be told and retold though his family knows them. As long as the children duck and tumble trustingly whenever he pinches an arm or cheek, he'll feel alive. As long as he complains, he'll never die. So it is that Goldstein's getting younger.

All of fifteen when he first outwitted death, called to serve the cause against the Kaiser, he broke his trigger finger with a loose brick pulled from a synagogue. Loyal to neither side, he fled his village for Warsaw where he met the widow Mikkelsen, who offered to put him up in return for work. She became his first attachment.

"Do you know I've never been with one so young before? And never a Jew."

"War makes strange partners," he concluded. His thoughts might drift, but her touch, the only blessing of the times, always led him back.

"There's a man with a thousand eyes who comes for me in my sleep," he still insists, pushing Poland from his mind, until it leaves him no peace. "I've tricked him since he first appeared. There were always plenty of others to keep him busy."

For awhile longer he might yet outrun the eyes. But Goldstein's finger is too hard a target to miss. He suspects it's useless to fight his appointed time, the settling of accounts. One morning it won't turn light in Bensonhurst. Then they'll lay him in the ground.

*

Although Goldstein's been in Brooklyn almost sixty years, his context is from the preceding score. Those in the family already in the ground, like finished chapters of his history, seem closer to his state of things as willing executor of life's dark business.

Each time he dreams of poison gas sinking in the cold of Poland, he's positive it's his time to go. *You've been handpicked for sure, so take your medicine,* he tells himself. All night he stays on guard, one eye remaining open— or else.

This morning he won't even hint at what he dreamt. Remaining in bed, he keeps his thoughts to himself without responding to any of his wife's questions which, by midday, drive him into the living room.

"Get dressed," she reminds him, already straightening her pearls. Made up with too much powder, her expression cakes. The face won't hold many of his insults.

Turning from his wife's voice, Goldstein shields his eyes from the incoming daylight. She leans toward him like a top that might unbalance and tip. It's a waiting room and he, a terrible patient, has become oblivious to everything except his own untreated, chronic ailment.

"Get ready," she insists again, talking louder to compensate for her deafness. For a moment they stare in silence, the resolution of fifty years, of unbridged differences.

"How many times do you have to tell me?" The lines crack deeper in his face, drawing from beneath it.

"You need to be reminded like a child."

"I could get more respect from a whore."

"What whore? You wouldn't know what to do with one."

"At this stage it's not a matter of knowing what to do, but whether I'd be able to. You've taken all the strength from me."

"Go find someone else. Be my guest. The more time you spend with her, the more peace I'd have," Hannah, backing away, assures him, the source of fifty years of aggravation.

"You don't fool anyone. What would you do without me?"

"Maybe I'll have to get myself a boyfriend just to find out."

"I've got just the man for you," Goldstein mutters, remembering. "He's got a thousand eyes and will proposition anybody. Would you accept his invitation if I should arrange it?"

*

The slow climb up the flight of stairs, stopping for air, hugging the railing while holding their hearts, tires them. For a long time neither can breathe slowly enough to exchange hellos. Kisses are put on their faces. His eyes glazed, Goldstein offers a handshake in the doorway and crosses the foyer. Their host lifts the coats off their backs.

Expecting great things of him, the children pull away as if to give Goldstein reason to chase when he extends his hand. He grabs for their arms with his bent finger they privately imitate, and pinches wherever he latches on.

Goldstein's daughter Rose brings drinks as he aims for the couch. The younger children scatter back to their rooms. The women sit around the dinette table, in a different conversation.

"I see you're still driving the big Buick," says Rose's husband, from the far end of the couch, the oldest boy between them.

"I'd give it to your son if he wants it. I'm ready to quit. My eyes aren't so good anymore." Their brightness doesn't dwell on his words. Goldstein turns mischievously on the couch.

He slaps the boy's thigh several times, then sticks his hand out to be shaken, pulling the boy closer, maintaining his tight hold. Talk in the dining room interrupts his thoughts. His staring at the women silently orders them to stop.

"Would you do your grandpa a big favor?" he asks. The boy nods.

Goldstein looks toward his wife, then back to his grandson, wondering where the years went, who stole them from his sure hold. Yesterday the boy was in diapers. It's been only weeks, it seems, since Goldstein first met Hannah. He curses under his breath at his luck.

"Can you find me a girlfriend?"

"What kind do you like?" asks the boy, smiling with the same mischievous eyes as his grandfather.

"Anything that walks. You think I could do better?" Goldstein winks at the boy and slaps his leg again. His wife is the only one not laughing, staying deaf.

"How about a nice forty-year-old?" baits the boy, leaning back satisfied.

"You know of one? What would I do with her?"

"You want me to tell you— at your age?" insists the boy, slapping his grandfather's knee.

Goldstein turns to the women, widening his eyes to play up the joke. The other, younger children, drawn out by the laughter, sprawl on the floor around their grandfather.

*

A woman of forty— what would Goldstein do with a woman of forty? Sixty years before, he was involved with a woman not far from forty. How old she looked then. Though he couldn't stand to look at the memory of the widow Mikkelsen anymore, the months with her were as much a part of him as Hannah's fifty years.

When he first entered her house, at a time when the Russian forces stood defiantly to the west of Warsaw, the one thing on his mind was keeping out of sight. That she provided for this was inconsequential to her. She wanted a man as much as the years of war wanted an end.

Believe me, he used to swear to friends, it wasn't hanky-panky I went looking for, but a place to escape the fighting. Although he loved the worldly things she taught him, she was a stupid woman, the greater ravaging of Poland, in his eyes.

"Do you lead every man who comes to your house to the bedroom?" he demanded of her, after the novelty of her seduction had worn off.

"The price of war," she said, faintly smiling. "Who am I to argue? Don't think I do this out of charity."

"What charity comes out of war? I still wind up

alone on the cot in the morning."

"Only after you get what you came for."

Whenever he desired her, Goldstein's mind drifted to her admission of having given herself to Polish soldiers. He imagined all those sweating men who had had her, and turned nauseous thinking of her flesh. All women had it in them to be whores, he thought, though when night came it all went so smoothly.

"Stay single," says Goldstein, now turning from his wife of fifty years back to his grandson. "A wife can posion a man. Look at me—evidence. I don't have long. She's seen to it."

Without looking, he takes a backhand swipe in his wife's direction. "Just close one eye for a minute—and goodbye. Stay single. Listen to your grandpa."

"Our wedding's set, three months from now," the boy announces. "It's going to last as long as yours."

"Tell me, is she pretty?" asks Goldstein. The boy smiles. His mother prompts a complete description from the dinette and is waved off.

"Does she have a grandmother for me?"

*

The bent trigger finger curls into an okay sign with the thumb as Goldstein smacks the table to make his point. At someone's attempt to divert the talk, he turns pale and straightens in his chair at the head of the table. He sits in a trance, brought along against his will.

As dinner ends, the children disappear and Goldstein, dabbing it against his tongue, lights his cigar. The host goes for a pinochle deck and pad to keep score, then shuffles and deals the first hand.

"Throw me a grandmother," says Goldstein, playing trump he's called. He squeezes his cards closed and slaps the table, releasing all his animated impatience.

"Enough foolishness," demands Hannah, as she studies her hand.

"You know I had a bad night." His face whitens, recalling. "My insides still hurt," he claims, cradling the cigar in his hook of an index finger as a series of coughs erupts.

"Why didn't you say something?" she asks, looking away. "We'd have stayed home." Her hands lie flat, palms down, one across the other against her cards.

"If papa didn't complain," reminds Rose, bringing him a drink, "I'd think something was really wrong." She places the glass in his hand. He lifts it to his mouth like medicine, wiping the fizz from his nose when he's drunk.

"Your lead," encourages Hannah, picking up her cards. She flaps them open like a fan.

"I'm still talking about last night," he shouts. The children are at the edge of the hallway listening. "I couldn't sleep. The man with a thousand eyes visited." Some slight leverage would pop Goldstein's eyes from their sockets.

"He's a smart fellow, but I told him, 'This is Goldstein you're talking to. I know what you're after.' It's his next time he comes," he pledges, rolling the cigar between his fingertips. He starts to smudge ash against the side of an empty teacup, but stops when Rose notices.

"Now I'll have to ask him another favor— to see my grandson's wedding. But who knows if I deserve it. I see his eyes too often. We've talked on a first name basis and still he won't take my wife as collateral." He widens his eyes, then winks.

"You'll be at my son's wedding and at the wedding of his son," insists Rose's husband.

"I'm a marked man," explains Goldstein, raising his voice again, against disbelief, making sure Hannah can hear.

Some sixty years before he was already a marked man, his bandaged finger masquerading as something innocent. Constantly he feared he might be questioned and found out.

Toward the end of the war, as the battered Polish countryside scabbed over, Goldstein informed the widow Mikkelsen he was a spy for Slovaticher Demotchover— merely the name of his mother's one-horse village. He swore her to secrecy before he told how he had infiltrated the Kaiser's lines, making off with military plans. The finger was his oath to silence, he boasted, if ever caught.

"Soon I'll be called away," he told her. "I might go just the way I came, with no warning. It's that way with wars."

"It's only that way with men. No one keeps you here, but you're safe with me as long as my children need a man to learn from."

"What they need is a father. I'm old enough to be a brother to them, no more. And to you, not even that."

"Like your finger we'll remain on your conscience all your life. Nothing you do will ever let you forget," she insisted, when she saw he had made up his mind to go.

"Throw," implores his wife. "Play the game." Grimacing, he comes out of his silent recollection.

The hand has gone around the table. He follows suit. His crooked finger remains wrapped around the burning cigar. Smoke camouflages his face, covering up the helplessness in his eyes.

*

In the last three months, Goldstein has seen the end too many times, too vividly. His time has come. Nothing will convince him otherwise.

Thinking all along he wouldn't make it, he now lays out his best black suit over the couch, stretching a tie at its side, for his grandson's wedding. His overcoat hangs from the bedroom door beside Hannah's dress in plastic.

As if setting out his clothes still isn't enough to ensure anything, Goldstein decides he must call to confirm directions. Remembering his son isn't far from the caterer, he looks up the number. They haven't spoken in many weeks.

There's the usual surprise then apology for the absent son. Goldstein, in the kitchen, picks on a stale roll as he listens to his daughter-in-law.

"I'm not sure I'm able to drive today," he says. "You never can tell if you'll see me." She assures him everyone is looking forward to it.

Dressing in the bedroom, Hannah picks up the extension and is about to dial when she realizes her husband is on the line.

"I thought for sure it was over last night," she hears him admit. "'Goldstein, get ready,' I hear the voice say. The only trouble is it doesn't tell me when. So I guess I'll see you— it'll be my pleasure." The two hang up, unaware of the third party.

Hannah puts down the phone last and shifts back confused against the headboard. Maybe he's keeping a girlfriend after all, she guesses. She closes her eyes and lets her weight fall freely into the firm mattress. Her ankles hurt from her present doubts. She unlaces her shoes and lets them drop beside the bed. Sure he's talked, but she's never found any evidence before.

She hears Goldstein walk from the kitchen to the bathroom, then listens to him hawk, the familiar sound that testifies against him. When she hears her husband nearly gag, she pictures his face turning red as the hand with his war trophy leans flat for support against the sink. As he begins coughing again, she listens for the first clear slap, his hand beating on the countertop, a cause of annoyance she's endured for fifty years.

Rolling from her back onto her side, she turns away, following the flight of thoughts beyond this life, beyond the room.

HARVEST OF GOULD

They spoke of gardens with as much civic pride in this suburb as of the historic town hall, or the railroad depot built a century before. On seeing the carefully tended, welcome green upon returning from the city, most people were relieved they lived where such things were still possible, beyond the spreading urban blight that had choked surrounding townships.

Before another diesel engine docked during the rush hour home, the passengers all knew to look for one large lot fronting the right of way. Their faces pushed against the grimy glass. A few waved, but only their reflections waved back.

Gould never watched them anymore. If he ignored them, he found the monstrosities went away faster, taking their foul odor, dust and rattling with them, tracks subsiding. He feared those fatal, metallic coughing seizures, as each train collapsed into the station, might inflict unseen disease upon his garden. But his vegetables grew unaffected, hardy as the shrubs and weeds that lined the tracks.

No day began without Gould fussing with his plants, watering and talking to them before the sun became insistent. Long before the first train came, he inspected every foot of his bountiful grounds. But if, as they passed, the commuters strained to see beside the house, they would have found the one pale specimen that spoiled the picturebook growth. Gould set her up on the chaise longue under the trellis every morning.

As his wife's health steadily declined, he divided his days between her and his precious plants. The growing season progressed and still he gave her equal time, moving her to make her comfortable or preparing meals, though it cut into his gardening. At her insistence, he left her to her book most of the day. He took a break when he remembered.

It was mid-summer when she took her turn for

the worse. Gould inquired about a live-in nurse. His wife called for him more often now, but he grew slower to look up at her shaking, less capable body. Though she waved her arm and tapped her cane for his attention, as often as not he didn't hear her over the garden's demands.

*

Years before, Gould had finished and divided the basement into rooms, thinking his brother would move out from the city and help him start a greenhouse. But when his brother died, the idea was abandoned, and the proposed bedroom became the pantry. Now the hired nurse, moving her belongings in, displaced the cans and jars.

The women sat together on the patio. The nurse set out the chaise longue now, helped Thelma into it, and pumped her with conversation in a way that hadn't recently been tried. Gould avoided their talk, bent over his vegetables.

He really didn't mind the nurse—his wife seemed pleased and he was free to work—until the day he briefly left his garden unattended and she entered it. As the nurse pinched back a crowded plant, he saw her from the bathroom and ran, tugging up his pants, outside.

"What're you doing?" Gould started for her. "This isn't a public thoroughfare."

"You should direct the growth. These could be doing better." As she backpedalled for the patio, she stepped helplessly on one of his plants.

"If I want your advice, I'll ask for it," snapped Gould, kneeling over the row she'd been up. "You have no business here."

Thelma's entire body shook as she sat forward, pushing off the chaise longue, inadvertently releasing its back. She formed each word carefully on her lips. "There are things you think you know that others may know better. Wyonne was only trying to help."

The nurse, eclipsing her in shadow, adjusted the chair and helped the winded Thelma to lean back.

Testing his patience, the women chatted on the patio every day while watching Gould work. When

Thelma napped, the other played solitaire and shouted suggestions to him as she spotted problems in the garden. He went about his business as if he didn't hear her, ignoring her advice until it was time for her to help Thelma inside, when he could take care of those very things without her watching.

His wife began to give advice as well and looked invigorated because of it. Talking louder to his plants, he continued with his tasks, and that kept their intruding spirits from his garden. He began to welcome the trains when they came knocking, banging, unwinding down the tracks like cats in pots and pans. Any noise was welcome if it drowned the chatter that went on behind his back turned squarely to the house.

But not all the distractions were as timely as the trains. A thunderstorm woke Gould one night. He sat sentry at the back windows, as though watching over a sick child, waiting for the fever to break. A sheet rain struck the house. He swore at the storm unable to see past it.

Something fell at the far dark end of the garden. Running outside in the rain half-dressed, he stepped in water streaming like thieves fleeing everywhere. The old wooden fence had tilted. Another gust would have pushed it down into the rows.

"How'd you make out with the storm?" asked the nurse, calling through the kitchen screen as she made breakfast and he salvaged as best he could what was damaged. She had heard him when she woke, had left a steaming cup of coffee on the patio. It sat untouched.

"We'll make it. Except the whole darn fence will fall if I turn my back on it." He looked it over, shook his head and spit.

"What you need is wire," she suggested. "Something that lets in the sun and you can run your vines up."

"My garden has gotten along just fine with wood." He straightened and turned from the house and her hounding shape in the window.

Muttering at the ground, Gould wondered how

he'd chosen her. He considered telling her to leave, but it was too close to the start of harvest. He couldn't think of firing her for another month or more. In the fall, he'd have time again to care for his wife. She could just get herself unused to this Wyonne.

*

The arrival of the six-foot-high wire fence coincided with a new low in Thelma's health. For several days, the nurse hadn't walked her onto the patio and Gould, putting the worst out of his mind, was relieved to be left alone without their nagging. All his attention went to his garden through its final stage, like a husband wanting to be with his wife as she gave birth.

The wire was left rolled at the side of the house overnight after the wood fence was taken away and the new foundation laid. Gould dragged up an old army cot from the cellar so he could sleep out on the patio. Allowing only a few moments to wolf down dinner, he felt indigestion clamp around his heart. But he couldn't leave his garden unprotected long—not now, with its defenses down.

"It might not help, but there's a new treatment they could try," recommended the nurse, the first words she had said to Gould in several days, since the fence went up and his concern had eased.

"She won't set foot in a hospital again, not after the last time, and I won't force her," he said, refusing to take sides with the nurse.

"Talk to her. See if you can convince her—for her sake."

Not about to be interrupted at length from his labor of love, Gould went on weeding. The fence caught the sun and lit up a circuit from pole to pole around the garden. Such vigilance was magical.

Still Gould slept outside on the patio. Each morning he bypassed the nurse to check his sleeping wife, then set up the chaise longue, hoping she'd feel well enough to read and see him work the vegetables to their yearly conclusion. He talked in the direction of that empty chair without looking up at it.

Now when the trains passed, the passengers pushed to the windows to inspect Gould's new fence.

Some of the rows had grown so thick and high that riders could never seem to find the figure in the dirt down on his knees. Corn stalks soared above his head like towering sons, guarding against intrusion.

Although the occasional neighbor walked up to the fence and called to Gould, the intimacy of leaning over a wooden fence was gone. Wire better matched the mood of the old man.

*

Some claimed they saw him cross the tracks to relieve himself in the weeds, or squat behind the corn like a hunted animal. Some said he slept on the patio, fair weather or rain, to keep his distance from the nurse who'd run him out of his own house. Others were certain he had become part vegetable.

Intent on inventing their own version of the truth, some boys came up the tracks for a closer look inside the wire barrier. Armed with a spade, Gould waved it to chase them away. They laughed and came closer instead, pushing the fence like a spring, squeezing its squares, trying to draw him out with taunts.

Gould ignored them, his mind back on his work, until he saw one reach in through the fence then quickly try to hide something behind his back. He came after them and they took off on a run for the weeds across the tracks, each waving his trophy out of the garden.

As he came up behind the nurse in the doorway of his wife's room, he momentarily frightened her. She hadn't seen him in the house for days. There'd been a change in his face. Something unpredictable had surfaced in his eyes.

"That fence is nothing but trouble," he shouted.

The nurse looked across the room away from him. His wife's eyes opened at his raised voice, questioning this rude behavior.

"You're to blame," continued Gould. "You've even turned my wife against me. I don't want you in this house anymore."

Escorted by Gould with his spade, Wyonne went to pack. He planted himself in the doorway outside her room. She closed the door to get at clothes behind it and that finally moved him back. Pulling over a chair to stand on, he looked out a ground level window to check his garden until the nurse was through.

Before she left the house, she showed him all the medications Thelma needed, repeating her instructions when absently he shook his head. She made a list for Gould detailing her routine. *There were never so many details before she came*, he thought. She said she'd come back soon to check on Mrs. Gould.

Once the nurse was gone, he drew the shades to Thelma's room as if that would protect her in his absence. His wife was calling for Wyonne. He returned to the garden, sensing the boys again, nearby. She called again and he pictured her in bed defying life, denying breath its entrance, to get back at him.

Seeing the garden was in no immediate danger, he returned to her. Her voice withdrew when he entered the room. Her calling had emptied her. As he approached, she shut her eyes, but they remained fastened on him. He touched her arm to see if she would move. Summoning all of her remaining strength of will, she rolled onto her side, putting up her back between them.

*

It was barely light. The old man lifted his wife in his arms like a sleeping child, one arm underneath her head, one behind the knees. He carried her without resistance out of the house.

"You can help me, Thelma, just like you used to."

He put her down like a full sack of compost or peat moss on the chaise longue. Positioning her hands in her lap, he pulled a blanket over her legs, then stepped into the garden.

He clutched his hoe as he patrolled each row. He turned at every sound and imagined sound—a snap from the wind, a whistle through the bushes across the tracks from the breeze. Through the fence his eyes followed the trees down to the depot. When he imagined he heard Thelma call and turned to look, she still hadn't moved.

The early rush hour train was late slowing into the

station on its way to the city, as if already fed up with the long ride still to go. It snorted hot breath onto the tracks, steaming beside the platform, panting heavily from its last run.

As the commuters pushed for window seats, the sharpest eyes went after Gould and then the woman still in her bedclothes on the reclining chair. The gardener leaned defiantly on his hoe as the train went by and quickly shrank into the distant tracks. Returning to his work, he spoke tenderly of his wife to his vegetables, believing her presence again would help things grow.

The heat of the day was building and the sounds of the town murmured along the tracks from both directions. The last of the rush hour shuttles spat and coughed out of the station. His wife was still where Gould had placed her, leaning forward at the waist now, face over her lap. The last of the morning commuters pushed up against the glass to look, barely seeing past the glare into the garden.

Across the brightness, birds rose from the roof, dots of ink spotted against the sky. Gould straightened and cocked his hoe at the commuters. He gestured with it as if it were his fist, shaking it at the eyes trespassing through the shining squares of fence, no doubt envious of all he grew. Proudly looking back to share this triumph with his wife, he suddenly paled. His prize blossom, in the hot sun, she had already wilted.

RAINBOW MAN

Running red lights, he sped up each deserted stretch of street— nothing besides the occasional cab or bus— Sonny knowing where to slow his empty panel truck for cops. Settling an old score with the night, the day brightened the sky in stages, like a fighter piling up points round after round. Things looked better in the half-light, on the way to the store. A whammy in opposing traffic's eyes, the sun coming over the dash lit up his face.

At the terminal market, Sonny honked and crossed the avenue against the red, then pulled beside the bigger trucks, waving without looking at the platform. His German shepherd pressed its nose to the glass. A truck was being loaded under the foreman's directing voice. Carting crates of fruit, the crew never broke the chain Sonny imagined linked each to the next, prisoners on a road gang. He watched them sweat, cooling their mood, their strained faces like shades to private rooms. His dog, erect on all fours, barked at the procession until ordered down.

Sonny squeezed out from behind the wheel and slammed the door. The dog, sinking into its master's dent, spread along the seat.

"How's it going, Sonny?" asked the foreman. "I'll get some boys on your order right away."

"The usual. Wife wants me to retire now that I bought her a condo in Florida."

"You ain't never gonna retire. People'll stop eating first." The foreman's laugh showed his toothless gaps.

"What's to retire to?" With the smaller man inside his shadow, Sonny looked past him into the office and nodded. Tony's boss yawned and waved. Sonny set his coffee on the platform.

"I'd just love to see the day I can quit. But I got a wife and four kids who eat a truck like yours every week." Tony shook his neck to where some workers had begun to load and Sonny's dog barked.

The work kept up under the foreman's inspecting eye. They were still fresh and he wouldn't have to watch them closely until the sun rose higher, gumming everything to a slow motion of what it was at dawn. But by then most of the loading would be done.

Sonny finished his coffee and crushed the cup in one hand, chucking it into a charred metal can. He shouted at his dog to quiet down. Braced on all fours, it slapped its tail and pawed at the glass to get at the men who loaded the panel truck.

"You'd think I'd be used to coloreds," said Tony, nodding toward a worker who fell off the pace. "I can't understand how you stay in that neighborhood."

"They don't bother me," said Sonny, breathing through barely opened lips. "Working with fruit so long I become a rainbow man. Thirty years, Tony. Thirty goddamn years."

Workers' long shadows stretched like towlines from the docks. They came and went between the warehouse and the trucks, their faces showing every crate they hauled and stacked high out of sight of unforgiving sun.

*

Sonny was breaking in a new boy on the truck in front of the store, teasing reliable Oliver that anything the boy dropped would come out of his pay, when his wife arrived, went to the register and counted what was in the drawer.

"You been to the bank?" she whispered to Sonny when she got him alone, out of range of customers.

"This way's easier than running to the bank every morning."

"You're a big idiot. Gate or no gate, they still find ways to break in."

Not knowing him, Sonny's wife studied the new boy stocking bins from the full crates. Not knowing what any one of them might do to get their hands on this money, she recoiled at the thought. Her biggest comfort was the German shepherd sprawled out on its stomach, claiming its spot next to the register, head on front paws. But after fifteen years, it hardly could be expected to do much more than bark.

She saw, in the revealing morning light, the toll her husband paid, his dark thick lids and puffy face. But here he never seemed to tire or complain—no weaknesses in front of them—or was it for her benefit? For a big man, Sonny moved nonstop most of the day, so there was that pace to contend with too and match.

When her husband sat to take a breather, Oliver started in on him as he had done for more than twenty years. "That come from hanging around with so many Negroes. You're getting lazy as us."

"Why, pretty soon," he went on, "your wife ain't gonna tell us apart. Let the wrong man in some night."

"Your kind'll try anything," Sonny bantered, his eyes flipping back and forth from Oliver's familiar scarred face to one customer, making up her mind, then another going through the apples, throwing those with bruises back.

"Ain't no apple with your name on it," said Sonny.

"You wanna give fifty cent banana?" a woman asked, unsure in her broken island dialect.

"You want I should eat the part that goes over fifty cents? We sell by the pound. Pick a bunch and I'll weigh it for you."

When she started to argue, misunderstanding him, his wife threatened to throw the woman out. Sonny's eyes rushed to someone unattended by the nectarines, afraid the stack would be upset.

The unending flood of customers worked on his wife, adding aggravation. At the register, she tried to stay out of their way. Scrutinizing their every move might have been half-bearable had Sonny put in that air conditioner he promised, which she'd insisted on a few years before if she were ever to work there again. Now she was glad he didn't—Who needed another temptation for thieves?—though this part of the city was always hotter than anywhere else.

The heat, by afternoon, had soured her face. The hired boy was dead on his feet and Oliver, wiping his face with a paper towel, sat on the end of an empty crate. Only Sonny hovered over customers.

"What has marrying you got me? If I work in the store I see you, if not I don't. I should be a paying customer. You'd pay attention." But now he hardly seemed to hear.

This year, she told herself, *I'm going to Florida with or without him. No more worrying whether he'll come home. No more eating alone.*

She was up during a lull, announcing she was going home, she'd had enough. Sonny shook his head agreeably. He'd be here for hours, still. She could have foretold his dinner would be cold, the meat as tough as shoeleather by the time he shuffled in the door. It wouldn't surprise her either to see her husband drag himself half-dressed to the back and fall onto their bed just after eating.

*

Sonny beat the alarm up as he had for thirty years, seven days a week, and hunted for his pants along the floor. Bumping around in the dark, he stretched and scratched his barrel chest before pulling on a tee shirt. His eyes, shut tight—the day still without leverage in the darkness—remained swollen with sleep as he staggered into the bathroom, caroming off the walls and boxes: the bedroom, after all those years, having become their storage space, living in the same small apartment.

Whether he made noise or not, his wife rolled over, sensing his absence, her sleep lightened closer to waking. She heard him splashing water and the German shepherd whipping its tail against the boxes. But it was Sonny's spitting into the sink which gave her getting up incentive. As he cupped handfuls of water to undo his eyes, she called out from their bed, asking what he wanted for breakfast.

In the beginning, Sonny had prepared his own. But over the years she had become upset if he let her sleep, if she didn't fix something of substance for him. The way she figured, he'd eat some crap along the way to work if she didn't make him breakfast.

This time she grabbed him as he reached the door, his jacket almost up his second sleeve, and held on until he gave in.

"Eat something. The damn business can wait for coffee and eggs. A man with your frame needs to eat."

"Who asked you? Leave me the hell alone. It's like the store. You're always following me around."

"It's better if you're the only one there?" She dug her long nails in his arm when he tried a second time to leave. "You'd rather one of them worked the register?"

Once she got him sitting, she started in on Florida from the kitchen. "You don't get out before winter and I'm going down without you."

"Yeah, I heard that before." Lifting his eyes, he continued flipping through a newspaper. "When are you gonna fix those eggs?"

"When are you gonna get out of there? It's a jungle. Worse every day."

"I'd leave tomorrow if we had a son to take over."

"If we had a son, he'd go to college."

"People got to eat." Sonny sat up impatiently in his seat. "I pull in more than these kids ever will."

"I'll never get you to Florida. I'd be like a widow."

She followed him, clutching his paper, to the bathroom. Though the tongues flapped out, his workboots stayed on, unlaced.

"What about that guy who wanted to buy the store the other week?"

"You call that an offer? What he's quoting ain't worth listening to."

Pressing up against the sink, Sonny began to cough uncontrollably. His wife backed against a towel rack, afraid to touch him in this violent, shaking state.

"These people are eating your soul."

"Just my fruit."

"Big shot—all you know is fruit after thirty years. Think about us for once. I never asked for much."

"Then you got more than you asked for. No one's stopping you. Go to Florida. Go tomorrow—I'll join you."

"Who'd be alive by then? A mule gets used to working with his back. It doesn't matter he has a brain."

"I'm going to work. Don't come in. Do me a favor." Sonny forced her and the dog out of the way, then shut the door.

She now concentrated on his breakfast. The apartment became silent, the couple unable to go another round. Her back was to the dinette when he returned. He heard her huff as she leaned into the counter and hid her face behind an open cabinet above the stove.

*

Sonny, seeing he'd be late in getting home, sent the new boy up the avenue for takeout, a bucket of fried chicken and some fries. Only he and Oliver, taking a final inventory of the bins, were in the store during this welcome calm.

Finished sorting bills and stuffing bands of them into a canvas bag beneath the counter, Sonny pulled a fishing knife out of the register drawer and peeled half an apple for the German shepherd lying at his feet. He bit into the other half, figuring the boy had been delayed with his dinner.

Oliver looked up, undoing his apron, as some customers came in. "You want me to stay?"

Sonny waved him off, apple in hand.

By the time the last customer was rung up, Oliver had heaved his jacket over his shoulder and picked up his newspaper and a bag of fruit. He stopped at the checkout counter where Sonny sat, cutting a casaba melon in two, and offered him half.

"Where's that damn boy with my dinner?"

Two men came in, the second kicking the doorstop to the center of the store, slamming the door behind them. The first shots knocked Sonny back against the wall, blowing apart a shelf of fruit and bags, the bin splintered from the blast.

Oliver dropped his melon and ran for the back of the store. A second volley followed him. When the German shepherd, growling, dashed out from behind the register, the sawed-off shotgun met the powerful leap in midair.

"Bastards...." Sonny staggered to his knees. Blinking blood, his eyes went after his attackers. Somehow he hurled himself up to his feet and lunged with his fishing knife, drawing wild retreating fire.

Undeterred, he didn't go far—just far enough to move them out the door. When he turned to scan the store, he spotted Oliver lying with his jacket up one arm, doubled over in the sawdust on the floor.

Sonny slumped against the register. He felt for the canvas bag, still there, beneath it. His mind, relieved, drifted from the holes disfiguring the walls to the row of faces, becoming blurred, pushing curiously against the plate glass. As his breathing changed, he still clutched the knife, until all feeling left and he passed out.

*

Of the pellets lodged in Sonny's head, two were left, close to the brain. The doctors could only point to his enormous luck. Recovery, they said, wouldn't be quick. The headaches, like nagging, he claimed, from a hundred wives, could last indefinitely.

His wife, who cried whenever she looked at his head dressing, pleaded, "Get some rest. Don't worry about anything. You'll kill yourself if you try too much."

"But what about the store?" he mouthed his question, so she could make each word out on his swollen lips.

"I've taken care of everything. Don't think about it," she insisted. "We're going to find a buyer and go to Florida like we should of done. You're luckier than you think. It's that hard skull of yours."

Because of the throbbing in his head, Sonny was up, unable to sleep, that first early morning back at home. He popped some aspirins, then slipped his legs into his pants and finished dressing in the dark. The bandage wrapped around his head pressed like cold metal. He pulled a watchcap over it. Without washing, he carried his workboots quietly to the door, taking every precaution so that his wife, on the living room couch during his recuperation, wouldn't be wakened.

THE TENTH PLAGUE

Starker's thunderous call for service signaled trouble to the dinner customers, suddenly fidgeting, having sat too long. The two teenage girls he dined with, uninvited, by the window under the delicatessen's Star of David sat fastened, fearful, to their seats.

"If it's the bathroom you want, you don't need to ask," instructed the owner, leaning over the showcase on her meaty elbows.

When Starker slapped the table, causing chairs to back from meals, Rozie remained bent over the cutting board behind the counter. Showing total control, she worked quickly, coordinating both hands beyond what one might have expected of her. Stretched stockings fell over ankles and orthopedic shoes, fixing her to the floorboards.

Starker turned to the two girls. They were suddenly through smiling.

"See what being a nice guy gets me?"

Eyes which had been drawn to him from around the room withdrew. The girls leaned back, silent in their chairs, leaving dinners to turn cold.

"All I ask is to make a living," insisted the owner, wiping her hands on her apron.

"Make it three beers, Rozie. Whatever's cold."

Her staring him down before she moved was intended for the other customers, to let them know how she felt about serving him at all, this son of the neighborhood's biggest developer, who'd been buying up block after block, renovating old row houses, bringing in new shops, charging the new tenants exorbitant rents. The younger Starker always bragged that once they bought her out they'd convert the block into a supermarket. Finished slicing tongue onto a roll, muttering to herself, Rozie pulled a beer out of the cooler. She uncapped it and turned a glass over the top.

"Mr. Hotpants with the girls."

Shaking off the waiter, she pulled up her weight by the apron. Her meat-gristly hand brushed the hair from her round face, sticking slivers to her sweaty shine. It was a face that held firm, sparing no detail, a monument to hard work and perseverence.

She came around the showcase, shifting aggravation like weight, leg to stalking leg. Placing the bottle on the table in front of Starker, she added the amount to his bill.

"I said three beers, Rozie," He looked the bottle over and waved his hand at her, pretending she existed only as air.

"They're only girls. Maybe they'd like ginger ale instead," she suggested, examining their silence like a mother who expected them to finish what was on their plates. Standing up to his antics was working like an aspirin.

Starker stuffed the last bit of sandwich in his mouth and wiped his pastramied hands on his pants. He set the glass down and rolled the bottle on its bottom edge back and forth.

"You people—always pushing something. Who wants kosher anymore? I see Yeshiva boys," Starker claimed, pointing at the owner as she again became busy behind the counter, "buying hotdogs on the streets."

As he dabbed at a circle of spilled beer to keep it from spreading in his lap, she shook her head, but by then he was again more interested in the girls. Rolling her eyes to the ceiling, Rozie wiped her hands on her apron.

A customer had come in and was studying the menu on the wall, with its old prices crossed out and new ones crayoned in. Several who'd been sitting left, the ringing up of the cash register prompting gleeful gutteral sounds from the owner's retarded son, who continued flipping franks and knishes on the grill, grinning broadly.

"At least most Jews had the good sense to move away from here," sighed Rozie, looking toward the waiter's agreeing nod as he picked up the order she had just filled.

There was a time when her husband was alive, before she took it over, when the restaurant was always filled. People waited, backed up out the door. Everyone ate deli. Now the only crowd, unrecognizable at that, passed them by on the changing street, more and more unlikely customers who never stopped.

*

"Leave them," she decided, greeting her mailman no differently than on other mornings. "They're nothing but bills." He slapped the letters into a pile on the counter and left. She let them sit. They were no way to begin a day. Just recently she had received a notice of an increase in electric rates and another on the upkeep of her husband's plot. "Why not?" she had asked herself in front of her son who shook his head agreeably. "Everything goes up."

Ignoring his morning chores, her son motioned to the mail, shaking excitedly over something he had discovered. He stuttered something, spread the letters like playing cards against the counter and, lifting one out, held it up to the outside light.

Laying it out sheet next to sheet, Rozie reread the letter several times, the first out loud, before folding and stuffing the pages back inside their envelope.

Returning to her work, she sliced an outer rim of fat from a hunk of corned beef, then placed the leaner piece back into a smoking tray in the showcase. Picking at the envelope again, she repeated news she knew it contained as if she never would believe it. Her son smiled over her shoulder, mouthing her words, like a shadow.

The waiter's arrival interrupted Rozie's thoughts. Walking past, he hung his windbreaker on a wall rack and slapped a length-folded newspaper on the table beneath it. He snapped a black bowtie onto one collar so it flapped against his shirt. It was still too early for customers.

"Bad news?" he asked, reading her face. Her son, still listening, went to his station by the grill.

"A cousin's first time across," she said, holding the envelope with both hands at the corners, as if it were just received and she were afraid to open it. "The father was my first cousin. He died in the camps. Somehow his son made it to Israel."

The waiter snapped his bowtie closed and patted down his sparse gray hair. He sat with his newspaper at the rear table by the restroom. "He wants money?"

"No, but he doesn't know anyone in New York."

"He can stay with me," offered the waiter, flattening the wrinkles in his white shirt. It was thin and shone where it had been pressed.

Preoccupied, Rozie held up the letter like something either living or wet, not sure what to do with it.

"Such a face and he hasn't arrived," said Sid, turning a page of his newspaper with the wet tip of his forefinger. Rozie shook him off and he resumed his reading.

"Seeing relatives for the first time is one thing. It's the other business—his cockamamie claims."

Knowing she'd tell him in her own time, Sid got up to pour himself a glass of club soda and resat, slowly drinking. The fizz caught on the tip of his nose. He stretched the starched collar from his throat.

"The letter says he's coming to the United Nations. God's given him the solution for peace for Israel," she continued, finally, rubbing her eyes on the back of her hand. "Did you ever hear such bragging?"

In a day or so it seemed that everyone was talking about this cousin from Safed. Her neighbors spread the word. The waiter let details slip to regular customers, who in turn repeated them to shopkeepers along the avenue. Rozie was at once susceptible to their interrogating eyes and ears. But if nothing else, and for this she'd have to thank the *yentas*, it brought in customers.

The developer's son, upon hearing the news, was amazed at all the kosher eaters all of a sudden. He considered all the extra wear on the toilets and the floors.

"Maybe you started the rumor yourself," he suggested. "Anyhow, I've got to hand it to you."

"The fuss will pass," Rozie assured him. "If you

don't think so, maybe you and your father will make a decent offer."

"With all your gimmicks you'll still come to us. Jews run from a neighborhood faster than anyone."

Starker turned and sat triumphantly by the window across from a young woman feeding hotdog to her child in a stroller. Though his eyes were fixed upon the mother as she shifted in her seat, his mind was on his Jewish problem.

*

The unfamiliar car snapped Rozie forward as she hit the power brake too hard. The honking all around her nudged her on. "Do yourself a favor. Close for the day," Sid had warned her, offering to drive. But his advice was no match for her strong will. Now she wished he had come along.

If anything happens, it's my fault, she scolded herself, then talked to the car to steady it. Made up, her face felt luxury it hadn't missed in years, since George. Who was there in the neighborhood to impress anyway besides widowers?— and none eligible, by her standards. Between stop lights she tugged at her dress. Fabric that had shrunk over the years now stuck to her— more sweat than in an entire week behind the counter. She pinched where it itched.

At the airport, her thoughts were on the restaurant, recreating the way her son and Sid had surrounded the morning newspaper when she came downstairs, thankful Dina— "that lovely girl" from the luncheonette, the only other Jewish store along the avenue— had come to fill in for her. Going over the flight in her mind now made Rozie doubt the details she knew cold. At least she had left explicit instructions, keeping her in charge of the delicatessen in her absence, somehow overseeing it with her concern. She breathed better knowing the plane business would be over soon. The dress could come off. The tight pumps, which she kicked under the seat first thing in the car, could go back in the closet, buried again.

As she waited for his plane, Rozie panicked that she might not pick her cousin out. If she did, there was no guarantee he'd return her nervous greeting with recognition of his own. What if when they found each other her thoughts ran ahead to the restaurant? This cousin would have to understand. Only then, and some reassurance was all she wanted from the letter she unfolded, would their distance part.

*

Unlimited beer, with sandwiches, for all who sat with him was Starker's treat. After several rounds, his eyes measured the room like a ring where he would meet his next opponent. "I'm giving three to one he don't show," someone offered. Starker flexed his laugh like biceps.

She tried to become inconspicuous, but everytime Dina began a sandwich, the developer's son slipped behind the showcase and insisted on showing her how.

"Haven't I watched Rozie enough? Jews shouldn't be working today, not on Moses' arrival," he said, instigating howling support.

Without Rozie there to run them into the street, the young boys teased her son and climbed onto the counter, caught up in the festive mood. Sid asked the men to set an example—regular customers were being frightened away—and for it someone grabbed him by his bowtie, pushing him aside.

All eyes were suddenly on the car pulling up to the curb, drawn to the stranger in the caftan as he slid from the front seat. Arms crossed, Starker straightened in the open doorway. Only his face was out of the sun.

Circling the hood to join her cousin, Rozie scanned the curious faces filling their path. Her eyes asked many questions and found answers quickly in the silence. Her son's expression as he flipped hotdog rolls toasting on the grill couldn't mean anything good. Sid's face, too, hid something he couldn't speak about yet.

"So this is your cousin," roared Starker, stepping aside. "Pretty authentic, but he looks more like an accountant than Charlton Heston."

Rozie ignored him as she reached over the counter

and took hold of her son's hand, tearing his attention away though his other hand, like a placemark, remained by the grill. Made to greet his cousin, he smiled through the introduction, forgetting his knishes and his franks. Sid was introduced next, then Dina, who was still as pale as when they first walked in the door.

"Hey, Moses, that the dress you gonna wear to lead your people?" Starker, slapping his hand against his thigh, stood a good head taller than the bearded guest.

"Show respect when you're in my store," demanded Rozie. Her anger flexed, testing the seams of her dress at the hips.

Starker's fists closed as he squinted in his stupor past the woman. Sandwiches and drinks were put down across the room. Customers braced, leaning toward the door. The Israeli smiled at the developer's son, diverting his temper, a scrawny tree withstanding a terrible wind.

"Enough of your bullying people," instructed the waiter, a step behind Rozie who was shooing Dina to the door.

"Maybe your God will send someone man enough to make me," answered Starker, backhanding air at the Safed Jew, staring him down.

Silent and smiling, the visitor gave no ground, keeping Starker at his distance.

"You should rest after such a long flight," said Rozie, grabbing her cousin by the wrist. Then she steered him out of harm's range.

Starker emptied his bottle of beer. Stepping victoriously into the street, followed by some of the men, he spit on the sidewalk next to Rozie's borrowed car before crossing the avenue to the bar on the other side.

*

Seeing Dina leave her parents' luncheonette, Starker stepped outside, started his car and followed her down the avenue. There were still plenty of pedestrians on the streets. Many stores remained open late.

When she turned onto a residential sidestreet into the shadows of row homes and rustling leaves, he turned too and drove ahead to the spot he knew she would end up, another two blocks down. He shut the engine and sat back. The street was quiet and becoming dark. His arm extended over the top of the front seat, over the imaginary shoulders at his side.

When he saw her in the side view mirror, he got out of the car with a sureness that belied his drunken state. Grabbing her arm, he shook her toward him. He put a hand over her mouth when he felt her start to scream. His heavy breathing frightened her though she struggled and kicked. He slapped her face but wouldn't hurt her, he said, if she behaved.

His hands were all over her as he forced her into the darkening house. Having already felt his anger, she didn't scream. She didn't give any of herself into what happened next. It felt to her like seeping darkness. Finally, he had enough and left through the same dark hall.

Starker, once home, kept trying to remember the girl's face, but the bearded one appeared instead. The smile of that small Jew pressed large against his conscience, keeping him awake. Several cigarettes in bed didn't help relax him. Lying in the dark, he was convinced he had to make the luncheonette and delicatessen pay. They'd sell to him when he was through with them. Then there'd be no Jewish stores. *I'm getting tired of pastrami anyway*, he told himself before sleep pinned him.

Near morning, the developer's firstborn woke burning with fever, sticking to his sheets. Though he could sense death coming in his restless dreams, there was nothing to be done. Something warm filled his mouth. He tasted blood and sat right up, staggered to the bathroom. His spitting blood into the sink frightened him. When he urinated to relieve the throb of his full bladder, it came out blood too.

He panicked as the strange aches spread and passed throughout his body. His nose ran without provocation, a bright blood stream that wouldn't stop. His sight was gone, but his memory of recent events left him no peace. The hell he housed burned for release from every pore, like open wounds that drained his life.

*

In the apartment over the delicatessen, as its owner and her son slept soundly in their beds, a small Jew from Safed wiped a wood staff clean with the end of his caftan in the spreading kitchen light. He planted a kiss at its crown, held it up outstretched before him, then placed it back inside its cloth wrap and secured it well.

SILVERMAN'S TOMB

It's Silverman again from his open window, coming in clearly across the courtyard. His relentless voice ignites another night, guts every airing apartment. Someone can't sleep, he winds up at his window watching Silverman.

By morning, Silverman still hasn't moved.

At any sudden sound out of the building—whether the water pipes or the flush and settling of a toilet, maybe the Ramoses fighting next door—I think of Silverman and go to look. I rub my eyes and swear I see him stepping inside from the ledge.

Reminding myself he's not your ordinary neighbor, I open a cold bottle of beer and wipe the short night's sleep from my eyes with fists I ought to shake at Silverman. How in heaven's name my wife sleeps through it is beyond me.

Looking again—his kitchen light's still on, but his chair's empty—I wonder where he's gone, scratch my head, wonder whether he was even there, whether I'm dreaming. I wonder if Rose—he always pleads and calls to her, romancing her with Yiddish songs—has managed to quiet him, get him to sleep. If so, I'd hate Silverman more for sleeping when I can't.

Everyone complains and no one does a thing. Talking to him is useless. He doesn't seem to hear. When he's not lecturing, the radio's always on. Boys hurl eggs at him before someone chases them out of the courtyard, but the sixth floor's out of easy reach of most arms. Occasionally, the mailman or someone from Social Security yells up to the top of the building, but Silverman never looks down. He never sees the pigeons, landed on the roof above him, cooing and shitting on his kitchen sill. Somehow I can take his talking longer if I think of it as an act, as a kind of ventriloquism by one of the birds.

"Don't you ever shut up?" I shout up from my open window, having had enough. "Someone's gonna make you eat your words."

Laughing, Jackson at his window even with mine says that words would be a hell of a lot better than what Silverman's already eating.

"Whaddaya mean?" I lean farther out the window until my eyes have nothing but four flights of air to consider.

"I've seen the old coot's apartment."

"You're full of it," shouts Mahoney, a flight above me, leaning on his big white knuckles. His proof positive smile is taken back as Jackson's middle finger aims at him. Mahoney's about to explode: fists lowering and filling with strength, stomach dropped, pushing against his tee shirt and belt in my direction.

"I tell you I've seen his apartment." Jackson folds his arms.

At last Silverman's napping. His head seems unnatural thrown back, tilted toward one side. His mouth's open and I smile when I imagine one of the pigeons getting off a lucky shot.

Mahoney waves a big disagreeing hand at Jackson, who's dancing to that disco crap of his. I make a mental note to break the freakin' forty-five into a zillion pieces, like I'd enjoy doing to Jackson some days for all the trouble he starts.

Jackson gives Mahoney the finger again, but this time the big guy makes a fist and pumps it up in the air, stirring the blood into his hand, as if forcing a space for the fist to fit.

"Goddamn you. I catch hold of you and your ass is grass. Nobody's been in Silverman's. Nobody's been in or out of there in months. Not even Silverman."

"So how's he eat?" I ask, unable to see around Mahoney's overhanging gut for a glimpse at his face.

"Paint chips. Pigeon. How the hell should I know?" I hear the voice coming around the belly. "Maybe he's got a shitload of cans. You know—like them fallout shelters."

"Enemy pigeon at twelve o'clock." Jackson's voice changes for this imaginary plane of his, and then he turns and guns for pigeons on the roof.

Mahoney's straw-white hair could catch on fire

from the deep red spreading through his face. Giving Jackson the finger back, one from each hand, he tugs his pants up at the belt, forcing up his fat like a balloon—like a big tit from below if one uses a little imagination.

"I figure his wife's still taking care of him." Mentioning this, I take their murdering minds off each other.

"Didn't she split?" asks Jackson.

"Committed, I heard, but she must've walked out of there." My hands braced on the windowsill allow me to lean into my arms and answer confidently.

"Silverman, Silverman—who the hell cares?" rants Mahoney. "It's the goddamn punks messing things up." He points accusingly across the way.

"Suck mine," answers Jackson, threatening to pull open his fly. "If you can lift it, faggot."

Mahoney stands full-height, pushing off his hands, and bumps his head on the windowframe. Jackson claps and swings his head in time side to side. His motion, not to mention Silverman's constant chattering—thank God he's napping—offer proof the building's become a zoo. The hallways always stink like monkey piss. The super doesn't care. Except I think it smells worse lately—blame summer. The bigger game are made nervous by Silverman's hyena laugh and ranting Yiddish. Their eyes stalk him. Tempers feed on his words. Appetites grow, clamoring for blood. Like predators who've tasted it, they now gang up on the weakest prey. Cornering him, they prepare for the kill.

But Mahoney's heart's set on Jackson, who'd slit his throat as soon as look at him if they ever run across each other in the building. For now, it's threatening gestures and obscene shouts across the courtyard, until I remind them that children—"my kids, dammit"—are down there listening to every word, repeating the worst when they come home, and they shut up.

"What's the place look like?" I ask Jackson, putting my foot up on the sill, and pump down more cold beer.

Heads come to their windows along the public domain of the courtyard. I can imagine most of the building listening, the many unseen ears cupped behind brick. Someone's face peeks through curtains. Someone else spreads wet slacks out to dry on a windowledge, deliberately avoiding my eyes. Someone looks down into the courtyard for her child—my boy's age—and waves at me, quickly looking away when I refuse to smile. Another woman shouts downstairs for her daughter, repeats the name, louder each time, until the child finally calls back, whining not to be taken from her game.

"The old man's apartment ought to be condemned. It and fat boy's stomach." Jackson looks up for Mahoney, but he's gone from the window. "Some say he's supposed to have a fortune hidden somewhere. Some say...." He nods, his guarantee.

"A fortune? Where?"

"That's all they say. I ain't seen it."

"People who talk to themselves are supposed to have money. You superstitious?" I feel the eyes from every window go from my words to Silverman, still sleeping, as if training weapons on an eventual target.

"It ain't fair for him to have so much and keep it for himself. There are plenty of guys who'd know how to spend it."

"You for instance?"

"You're reading me." My neighbor polishes his nails against the front of his shirt, then blows into them. "Maybe he's asked to be buried with it, like them pharoahs. Ain't nobody gonna get their hands on it."

Silverman rich? It doesn't seem possible. I'll check with the super, see what he knows. Might be he's been up there to spray or something. Maybe my wife's heard something from one of the women.

Wait a minute, Silverman talks. There's got to be a code word, something in his mumbling or his yelling for no reason, or maybe in the dumb instructions to his wife he's always repeating. Rose, yes Rose. Somehow that's got to be it.

My ears perk up, fitting the pieces.

Jackson's not talking, but maybe he hasn't figured out as much. Hell, I'm not gonna be the one to tell him.

I'm waiting, Silverman. Go on, spill it. Speak English, old man. Give me your money and I'll go easy on you. It's either me or a dozen others in the building. Jackson'd mug his own mother for a dollar. That's how I figure he's never been to see you.

"Where do you go without me, Rose?..." It's Silverman again. His eyes are closed. He's making faces like he's two people carrying on a conversation. "...Why bother me with such things? Okay, make herring instead of borscht. Kill me with pickled..." Make a note of that, I tell myself.

Silverman's eyes open. He stares straight ahead. "...I'm afraid for us. The building's turning colored, Rose. I'm afraid should you go out alone, should someone hurt you. Who can live another day among such people?"

I ask myself, That's living?

*

I'm possessed by this fortune. My wife threatens me with divorce if I don't come away from the window, if I continue to take days off from work, if I don't keep my mind on her when we're in bed, if I ignore the kids or stay this irritable another day. I'm filled with the nonsense that spills out of Silverman, wanting better for us all. I'm fed up with living this way, here.

I break off a beer from a six-pack. The face I return with incites arguing.

"Is it going to fly in the window?"

"Shut up."

"Is it going to drop out of the sky?"

"Enough. Enough of this. We're gonna be very rich very soon."

Claiming I need air—"So go back to your window," she tells me—I leave the apartment, leave her shouting after me. I'll show her.

I climb the stairway up to six and stand with my ear to his door. Silverman sounds like the treble inside a speaker. I station myself there a long time until someone comes up the stairs, dragging feet, and I hide by the incinerator. The steps cross the tile hallway and a door closes at the far end of the floor.

Again I'm positioned at the old man's door, cupping hands between it and an ear. I try the doorknob. To my amazement it's unlocked. Goddamn that Jackson. He wasn't lying. I kick at the hallway and shush the wall's hollow echo. I look behind me and listen, stopping my heart, for anyone coming. My hands are cold and sweaty, so I rub them up and down my pants legs many times.

Silverman's still talking, competing with his radio. But where's Rose? Is she on the other side of the door, barely breathing so I can't possibly hear, waiting to lunge at me with a kitchen knife? Maybe there's a dog just waiting for a leg so he can chew it off, tear me to shreds like a stuffed doll.

My pulse races as I grip the doorknob, deciding, listening for Silverman to drop a hint of the kind of attack to expect. But I'm deaf to anything but the fortune I imagine inside. If Jackson's been here, others must know about it. Then again, maybe it's some kind of trick and I've become Jackson's number one sucker to fall for it.

Has anyone, I wonder, really been in Silverman's apartment?

Twisting the doorknob hard, I push slowly, slower when the door begins to squeak. Silverman's still ranting and raving about the building changing, about his wife leaving. It sounds more believable when you can't see him. Rose will greet me at the door, no matter what I want to think. My fists close, tighten, drawing blood to them, drawing all my strength into my hands.

The door opens enough. Bright light veers through the vertical crack into the darkness of the sixth floor hallway. My heart cringes like a bird held against its will, struggling to be free. I put a hand to my chest and push to keep it from flight. Footsteps and children's voices climb the stairs, getting closer. My own son's voice is among them. I step inside the apartment and slide the door behind me, fronting the foyer. Pinning my back to the door, I close it quickly.

Silverman's going nonstop at the window now, as if he suspects an intrusion. My hands hang ready at my sides. Feet spread, cold. Quietly I take one step and stop, then cross the foyer cautiously. I feel better as he keeps his madness up, knowing he rarely stops, not sure what I'd do if he did. But if he'd scream, who'd notice? Silverman's usually loud.

The bedroom's been through a war, I swear. The mattress, gouged, loses stuffing from each cut. Again I think of Rose coming at me with a knife. My head whirls after an imaginary attack.

There's an invisible weight sleeping in the bed. The sheets, tea-stained, are slit into confetti, scattered not so cordially as dust. Except for a dresser that's been taken apart—many times, from the looks of it—there's no furniture. Several emptied drawers are on the floor, the others pulled open. Clothes are spread everywhere with newspapers and books, mildewed Jewish books with their covers ripped off. From the looks of it, the newspapers could've been used to train a dog.

Where it hasn't already peeled, the ceiling hangs in strips ready to fall, hit the wooden floor and splinter. Each wall's dirty and cracked, marked with chalk and pen telling who's been here. There isn't a single lightbulb in the room and wires curl exposed from the ceiling where a fixture should be. Even the switchplate's missing. The window's nailed shut to its frame.

I imagine hiding places in the walls and floorboards that haven't been tried. Still hearing Silverman at his kitchen window, I kick through his stuff, squinting and coughing into my sleeve like a prospector deep inside the earth.

Silverman's mouth doesn't stop.

*

"What's the apartment like?" I ask Jackson, next time I catch him at his window staring into the courtyard. "Locate any buried treasure yet?"

"Silverman's? Yeah, I been inside the place." He gives me a look, like he's figuring out what I'm up to. "Don't believe all the stories you hear."

"Whaddaya mean?"

"I don't know anyone who'd live here unless he had to."

"Or had no place to go." I follow the flight of pigeons to the roof. "Hell, old people are hiding money all the time. Some don't trust banks. Maybe Silverman keeps it in his mattress."

"Maybe Silverman's not talking," decides Jackson, snapping fingers as he turns the record up. His eyes flicker closed, extinguishing the only light in his face, and he begins performing like a peacock.

"Silverman's always talking, but saying nothing." My voice rises above the music. Heads pop suddenly from their windows throughout the courtyard, Mahoney's too. I hear his window pushed as far up as it goes.

"Always assume someone's smarter than he sounds," cautions Jackson. He leans into his windowsill, staring at Mahoney. His veins surface and it's like looking into his arms. There's a tattoo on his bicep I've never noticed before, something like the mermaid my wife's always wishing I'd never had done. She sees it, she'll be telling me Jackson and I have a lot in common.

"You guys gonna knock it off already with that fortune crap?" screams Mahoney. "Someone's gonna get hurt with talk like that. Some of these bastards believe it."

"Suck mine," I find myself saying to him.

He spits down from five, but I duck inside as he gets off the shot. Jackson rolls his eyes. Silverman's stirred up and talking faster, louder in the commotion. I grab my wife's favorite ashtray—a gift from her aunt—set myself and hurl it out the window at Mahoney. It strikes brick, smashes and falls to bits into the courtyard and children below.

Mahoney mutters, "Dumb prick." Shutting his window, he rattles glass. I stay out of range of retaliation.

Voices go up like a tinderbox I've lit around the courtyard. Mothers start in, giving me an argument. I find a different curse for each. My wife too—one second she's screaming and the next she's beating on my back until I've had enough: enough of her swearing and her threats, enough of Jackson's laugh and Mahoney's lip, enough of this tenement pisshole with its yelling every-which-way in sixteen dozen languages, enough of Silverman and those pigeons cooing like they've nothing to do with all of this. I slap my wife hard across the mouth, drawing blood and tears.

"Drop dead." She covers her lips. Seeing the blood on her hand, she comes at me again like a fighter who won't quit, incensed at her injury.

I slap her again to the floor and this time she stays down, crying and still cursing me for the day I was born and the night we first met, for all my scheming and my lame excuses to get drunk, for all the times I couldn't get it up. Hearing that, I kick at her.

"Bastard, go to hell," she shouts, and only quits when I threaten to kick again.

Slamming the door out of the apartment, I serve notice to my neighbors, run through the hallway banging on each door. I leap up the staircase straight to six, to Silverman's door. Not careful this time, not worrying if I'm seen, I'm confident I'll find that money and shut them up once and for all.

Goddamn you, Silverman. This is all your fucking fault.

*

When I return, still fighting calm, my apartment's empty. I figure she's taken the kids over to her sister's on the bus. She'll come back—always does—never takes enough clothes. Hell, I'm gonna buy them all new clothes. This radio'll do for a start.

But there's no one here to applaud this line of thinking, only the walls, and they're turned silently against me too.

Bothered by everything, I fall across the bed. Suddenly warm, I jump to my feet and slide the window open wide as it'll go. I turn on the radio, placing it on the windowsill to show it off. That's only the start, my friends, only the start. It isn't even dark, but I want to sleep so I can dream and see the fortune grow.

Through the courtyard mothers call their young upstairs for bed. The babies cry like sirens. Someone's drums drown out the faintest voices. But nothing's lost, all sounds are counted in these final moments of the day.

My lungs fill with the building's rot—worse because the evening's still. This room's like beer gone warm and flat. I light a cigarette hoping to cauterize the air. Blood and sweat run from me in opposite directions, would conquer if they mixed.

The silence of the oncoming night's against me. I can't be still in it too long. I miss my children's commotion. I miss their mother. Any bad blood's hers. I turn the radio louder.

No lights on in this sweatbox, the windowspace grows dark as the walls. Tired of listening to music, my mind races across the night and back looking for a way out of the dark, for a single light to lead me safely.

I swear it smells like Silverman's ruined mattress, the stale air of his newspapers and books matted to the wood floor. Something vile's coming alive up there. I wonder if his floor could fall through, whether all the apartments are rotting in this heat and about to fall one on top of another. I rush to the window, planning my only escape from Mahoney on five.

It's quiet from Silverman's and has been for a long time. Pigeons parachute onto his kitchen sill. I turn the music loud as it'll go. I don't think I'll ever sleep. Something's screaming in my brain.

Sitting at the window with my bottle of beer, I light another cigarette. His fortune's as good as mine. I'll come back from six a respected man next time. More lights go on throughout the building, like features cut in a jack-o-lantern. No one can see me in this dark. I still hear kids out in the courtyard.

Wasn't that my son? Where's Jackson with his jailbait? Isn't that Mahoney's heavy footstep—Get outta my head—testing the wood? Damn him. The Ramoses are quiet for a change. Now they've done it—that little brat of theirs is always crying.

Someone there? "Who is it? Who's there?"

Oh God. Lower the radio, that's it. The window. Out the window— throw it.

Please, Silverman, leave me alone. You just stay the hell away from here.